# Magically Generated

Jackie Lau

First edition: October 2025

ISBN 978-1-989610-46-6 (ebook)

ISBN 978-1-989610-47-3 (paperback)

Edited by Ali Williams

Cover by Jay Pillerva

For Carla

# Chapter 1

Everything was a scam.

That's what it felt like to Nora Blackburn, at any rate.

Take the phone, for example. Once upon a time, her mother had taught her how to use it in case of emergencies. Her little fingers had struggled with the dial on the old rotary phone.

That phone—which had been replaced by the time Nora started kindergarten—bore almost no resemblance to the device that she currently held in her hand. She took it wherever she went, and she rarely used it to actually speak to people. When she did get a call, there was a good chance it was a scammer, and as a result, she almost never answered her phone when the number wasn't in her contacts. But she answered it now, only because she was expecting a delivery. "Hello?"

She was met with a recorded message that was almost certainly not from where it claimed, and she ended the call with a stab of her finger. She was even more frustrated with the world than usual today.

Since she'd finished work for the afternoon—she worked from home as a technical writer—she navigated to a social media app, even though it would annoy her further. She immediately saw a post spouting something utterly ridiculous.

Fake news. Engagement bait.

It never ended.

The signal-to-noise ratio on the internet was appalling. She had to be suspicious of everything she saw, and she was tired of it. Many things were mostly harmless—more annoying than anything else. Some were propaganda. Others were trying to get money or personal information out of her, and she couldn't afford to be deceived again; she had to remain vigilant. She didn't trust anyone but the few people who were close to her.

She came across a news article—yes, it was from a reputable source—about a tech company trying to do something that was clearly a terrible idea. Why, science fiction from decades ago had warned of this exact scenario! Did nobody read books?

When Nora was younger, she'd sworn she wouldn't become one of those people who constantly reminisced about the good old days, yet that's exactly what she was doing...and she was only forty.

But technology had given her one good thing: she could sign out books from the library without leaving the comfort of her home. She picked up her ereader. Soon, she had an old book from one of her favorite authors on her device. Excellent.

A moment later, the silence of her apartment was interrupted by a ringtone in the hallway. Specifically, the first few notes of "Deck the Halls." She wondered if the owner of the phone used that ringtone all year round, or if they changed it for December. Or maybe it was a ringtone just for one person on their contact list—a friend or relative who loved Christmas, perhaps.

Nora didn't particularly like Christmas. She wasn't quite the Grinch, but she'd long found the whole thing...too much. Crassly commercial at times.

And this was the first year she'd have to spend it alone.

It shouldn't bother her, given her feelings about the holiday and the fact that she spent much of her time alone anyway, but it did. She'd struggled with getting through the Christmas season ever since her mother had passed away almost three years ago, in between Christmas and New Year's.

She sighed as she got up to make herself a cup of tea. She was forever drinking tea in the winter because she was always cold. Not that it was officially winter yet, but it was December 2 and there was snow on the ground. A lot more would be coming soon, if the forecasts were to be believed. Ugh. The first big snow of the year always brought up bad memories of trying to rush to her sick mother's bedside as traffic screeched to a halt.

Her phone beeped, and this time, the message wasn't from someone who wanted her to click on a suspicious link. No, it was from her sister.

**Brianna:** I don't want you to travel in this weather. Next Sunday?

For Christmas, Brianna, her husband, and their two children going to Nova Scotia, where Brianna's husband had lots of relatives, so they'd planned to celebrate early with Nora. Just a small get-together this weekend. They were her only family now, and Nora had been looking forward to this dinner, but yeah, it made sense to put it off another week, especially since half of her nephew's gift still hadn't arrived—that was the delivery she was waiting for.

**Nora:** Sure! That's probably best.

She didn't express her disappointment. There was no reason to make her busy younger sister worry about her.

She set down her phone before flopping on the couch and reaching for her ereader again. A long weekend alone stretched before her.

The only positives? She didn't have a driveway to shovel because houses were too expensive, and unlike last December, she hadn't picked up a part-time retail job to replenish her savings.

She just needed to make it through the rest of the month. Sometimes, simply surviving was the best you could hope to do.

Yes, Christmas would not be merry for Nora.

Everett Sun took a break from decorating his tree and looked out the window. Snow had started falling. They were supposed to get at least 15 cm this weekend, then another 10 cm midweek.

Perfect.

Finally, he'd be able to put his plan into action. He'd been waiting for years, but there was never enough snow. Last year, Toronto had barely gotten any until February, and that was too late. But this year? Lots of snow before Christmas, and it wasn't supposed to melt anytime soon.

He whistled along to "Let It Snow" as he picked up another Santa ornament. He had quite the collection of Santa decorations. This particular one was a ceramic ornament of Santa getting stuck in a chimney. He hung it on the tree below a whimsical ornament of Santa reading a book to a snowman.

It was a little sad to be trimming the tree by himself. When he was a kid, they'd always done this as a family. But his family was on the other side of the country, and he'd told them that he wasn't coming home for Christmas this year.

What he hadn't mentioned, however, was the reason: he'd hoped this was the year he'd be able to execute his plan. He couldn't say anything because he'd never told them about his abilities. Nobody knew, in fact, and he had no intention of changing that, but he wanted to prove to himself that he could do something special with his magic.

As a kid, Everett had imagined it would be great fun to be Santa Claus. Not just because he wanted to have flying reindeer and eat lots of cookies, though that was part of it, but because it would be satisfying to bring joy to so many people.

Though he couldn't deliver millions of presents in a night, he could do something else.

Nearly all of his friends were married now—he'd gone to a wedding just last weekend—and many had children. They had less time to hang out than before, and so he had few social engagements these days, especially since he hadn't dated in a while. For whatever reason, none of his romantic relationships had worked out. He hoped that would change one day, but for now, it was just him.

It would be a good year to make his dream come to fruition, and maybe it would bring Christmas cheer to others who were lonely over the holidays.

Once he'd finished decorating the tree, he pulled out his old sketchbook and studied the drawings. It was important to memorize every detail—that was the key to executing this successfully.

A knock on the door startled him. Before going to see who it was, he shoved the sketchbook under the tree skirt.

Anything related to his magic would remain a secret.

# Chapter 2

Nora stared at the wreath on the door. It was filled with pinecones and baubles, and there was a big red bow at the bottom. It was infuriatingly festive.

The door swung open, revealing Everett.

Everett *Sun*. She hadn't known his last name until a minute ago, when she'd heard a noise at her door. She'd opened it to find a package. To her frustration, it wasn't the one she'd been expecting, but one meant for the person who lived across from her. She could have left it in front of his door, but someone on the first floor had apparently had a package stolen the other day, so she'd decided to knock. Besides, it was obvious he was home from the music.

"Hi, Nora." Everett smiled and adjusted the square frames perched on his nose.

The damn man was always smiling whenever she saw him, and in that red flannel shirt, he looked like an Asian Santa Claus. He didn't have a big white beard, but he did have a neatly trimmed black one, as well as a rather round physique.

It also looked like Christmas had thrown up in his apartment, which contributed to the whole Santa thing. Over his shoulder, she could see a Christmas tree with lights in a rainbow of colors. It was loaded down with ornaments, including a star that twinkled at the top. On a small table, there was a Christmas village set, sitting atop a cotton wool sheet that was meant to be snow. The lights in all four buildings were on, making it look like miniature families were cozying up inside.

Nora pulled herself together. She should stop assessing her neighbor's Christmas decorations and do what she came here to do. She thrust the cardboard box in his direction.

"This was delivered to me," she said, "but it's yours."

"Thanks." His grin broadened. He looked at her as though she'd done him a great kindness, even though she'd merely taken a minute to hand over a misdelivered package.

Rather than closing his door, he ripped off the packing tape and opened the box, revealing...even more ornaments.

"Perfect timing," he said. "I was just decorating my tree and...oh." He held up an ornament that depicted three reindeer having what could only be called an orgy. "This isn't what I ordered."

She arched an eyebrow.

"Really, it's not." He shoved the ornament back in the box and pulled out another one. It was a naked Santa figurine, but the naughty bits were covered by a large stocking. "Nor is this." The tips of Everett's ears were almost as red as his shirt. "I wouldn't have opened the box in front of you if I'd known what was in here. They must have given me someone else's order. The store sells lots of interesting Christmas décor."

He was clearly surprised and embarrassed, so she was inclined to believe him. Not that there was anything wrong with the existence of such ornaments, but opening them in front of a woman he barely knew? She might have worried about uncomfortable sexual comments.

Instead, he said, "Hopefully, they have decent customer service rather than a useless chatbot."

"Yeah, those can be terrible. I ended up going in circles with one the other day. But least you didn't travel to the store during a storm."

Though even as she spoke, she considered the fact that unlike her, Everett looked like someone who enjoyed being outdoors in winter, if there wasn't a snowstorm. He had a bit of a lumberjack vibe going on. Maybe it was just the flannel shirt.

He nodded. "I hope you don't have to go anywhere this weekend."

"No, I'll be home." She glanced at his tree. "Well, I'll leave you to it." Even though she hadn't intended it, her voice sounded a touch snarky.

Unfortunately, this didn't escape his notice.

"Do you celebrate Christmas?" he asked.

"Yes."

"But you're not a fan of it?"

"Not really. It's just...a lot."

A new Christmas song started playing from his stereo. He sang along softly, and she didn't join in. She couldn't believe she was being subjected to so much holiday spirit. Nora knew she wasn't being fair, but everything was getting on her nerves right now.

"You don't like bells or mistletoe?" he said. "Or tinsel?"

She shuddered. Tinsel was barely a step above glitter—and she was still finding glitter from the craft project she'd gotten from her niece back in April.

"What about the food? Candy canes? Cookies? Gingerbread houses? I have an extra advent calendar if you want one."

"Of course you do," she muttered. "Thank you, but no. I don't need a holiday to eat sweets."

"Snowmen? Snow angels? Sleigh rides?"

"Have you ever actually been on a sleigh ride? That's not something most people do."

"What about cuddling up by the fireplace with a mug of hot chocolate?"

"We live in a high-rise," she said. "I don't have a fireplace. As for the rest of it..." God, now she was thinking of snuggling up with *him*, and that wouldn't do. She blamed it on the orgiastic reindeer ornament, even if those reindeer were doing a lot more than snuggling.

"Let me guess. You don't need a holiday to make you cuddle."

"Precisely."

He didn't call her out on her obvious lie.

"Have fun with your Christmas tree," she said, trying not to sound snarky this time. And with that, she returned to her apartment and put the celebration of Christmas out of her mind.

But when she was wide awake at three in the morning—an increasingly common occurrence these days—"Jingle Bell Rock" was stuck in her head.

She sighed. Damn Everett. But at least that interaction had been real, unlike so many things in the world these days.

·❤·❤·❤·❤·❤·

"Should I meet up with him?" Aimee asked before sipping her decaf peppermint latte. They were sitting by the window at a coffee shop.

"You've been talking to him for a few weeks now, so...I guess?" Nora always struggled with giving romance-related advice. It really wasn't her area of expertise. "But don't tell him where you live. Meet him in public."

"Of course."

"If you need an out, just text me, and I'll call you with a convenient emergency. And if you go home with him, give me his address."

Aimee went through phases where she dedicated herself to online dating...and then she'd deleted all the apps from her phone...and then restart the whole process a few months later. A bad experience or three didn't seem to dim her hope that "the one" was out there somewhere. Not for long, anyway.

Nora, on the other hand, had given up. It was the logical thing to do after she'd fallen for a romance scam. She couldn't help thinking of that now—she'd met him on an app, more than two years ago.

"And if he..." She couldn't finish that sentence. She gripped her mug and tried not to imagine all the possibilities. There were physical dangers, as well as other kinds.

Knowing what was on her mind, Aimee reached out and squeezed her hand. Aimee was her best friend—her only real friend, in fact—and she was the sole person who knew what had happened to Nora.

Nora had been too ashamed to tell anyone else.

"Hey, did you see that snow sculpture?" Aimee picked up her phone and navigated to a picture on social media. "Isn't it cool that someone made this out of snow?"

Nora was thankful for the change in topic. She pulled the phone out of her friend's hand and took a look. There were two bears sculpted from snow, each gripping a hockey stick in their paws. They also sported toques, which was silly. Why would a bear need to wear a winter hat?

But that wasn't her biggest problem with it.

"Look at the bear's fur." Nora zoomed in. "It's clearly AI."

"No, it's not," Aimee said. "It's in a Toronto park."

Nora shook her head. "It's definitely fake."

"It's everywhere on social media today."

"Have you seen pictures from multiple angles, or is everyone sharing the same photo?"

"The same photo." Aimee sounded dejected.

People wanted to believe things like this were real, but there was so much garbage online. Seriously, what were the chances that such a snow sculpture would just appear?

That nobody saw the sculpting process or knew who had done it?

Yes, like the picture of hundred-year-old identical triplets that Nora had stumbled across the other day, it was fake. Though she felt bad about shattering Aimee's illusions, she couldn't ignore the issues with the image.

She drank her tea, but it wasn't enough to warm her.

Everett shouldn't spend so much time on social media. It wasn't good for his blood pressure. But dammit, he wanted to see the reaction to his snow sculpture.

Unfortunately, it wasn't quite what he'd hoped.

The first picture was suspected of being AI. The person who'd shared it had only posted a single photo, and they hadn't returned to refute any of the accusations. Though even if they had, Everett acknowledged that it might not have made a difference.

And so, in addition to all the people who thought it was cool, there were lots of people who thought it was fake.

Goddammit.

That sculpture was definitely real, thank you very much.

Growing up in the Bay Area, he'd had little experience with snow until his family moved to Canada when he was eleven. His Chinese American father had met his Chinese Canadian mother when she'd come to the US for university, and she wanted to return to her hometown.

In Victoria, Everett had…well, still not much experience with snow. Victoria got little snow compared to the rest of Canada. But when he was thirteen, there'd been a few centimeters of accumulation. He'd wanted to make a snowball, and somehow, it had just formed at the thought. He hadn't needed to pack snow into a ball, then roll it on the ground to make it bigger. Not, it had simply happened.

"Did you see that?" he'd shouted to his older brother.

His brother had shrugged. He'd been going through a phase where he was unimpressed with everything. "You made a snowball. So what?"

That was his only attempt to ever tell someone the truth.

Over time, Everett had realized that no one could actually see him work with snow, though afterward, they could see his creations. He'd also discovered that he could make much more impressive things than snowballs. If he thought very, very carefully about exactly what he wanted, he could make it happen. The snow, however, had to already be on the ground for him to work his magic; he couldn't conjure snow out of thin air. He'd practiced in private and destroyed his creations afterward, not wanting to draw any attention.

For university, he'd moved east, to somewhere that got more snow than Victoria. He started leaving some of his smaller snow sculptures up, hoping someone would enjoy them, and over the years, he'd developed a fantasy, of sorts.

A dream of making snow sculptures all over the city where he now lived. Uniting Toronto in a magical mystery, just before Christmas, as sculptures appeared at random.

He would have loved something like that as a kid. Some adults forgot what it was like to be a child, but he never had.

Alas, it wasn't going as planned.

Eventually, he came across additional pictures of the snow sculpture, taken from different angles. One of the pictures was a selfie, a snow bear's face in the background. But the algorithm wasn't sharing these photos. It favored posts that garnered outrage.

Well, no matter. Everett wouldn't let this stop him. He'd proceed as usual tonight.

His mind drifted to the white woman who lived across the hall. He couldn't help wondering if Nora had seen any of these pictures. After their conversation the other evening—the most words they'd exchanged in the two years he'd lived here—she kept popping into his mind at random times.

She seemed like the sort who considered smiling a weakness, and she'd never let herself smile around him, not once—the ornament mishap had only led to a raised eyebrow. He had the inexplicable urge to change that, even though he barely knew her. To show her some Christmas magic that would bring an unconscious smile to her face. It was a silly desire, but he couldn't help it.

Hopefully, she liked walruses.

Nora had run out of Scotch tape. She now had three options: she could use duct tape, she could put the presents in gift bags, or she could go out to get some more Scotch tape.

With a sigh, she admitted that the third option was the best.

Duct tape—the only tape now in her possession—would not make for very pretty gifts. Although she had a few gift bags, she recalled finding such things disappointing as a kid; they weren't as satisfying as tearing open paper. And while the holidays might not feel magical to her now, she did want her niece and nephew to have a good time.

It was eight thirty at night, but the nearest Shoppers would still be open. She put on her winter boots and coat.

The temperature was well below freezing, but it was a short walk, and at least it wasn't snowing.

As she locked her door, a delivery person approached. He carried a helmet in one hand and a very large order of food in the other. To Nora's surprise, he knocked on Everett's door.

Her neighbor lived alone. Did he have company?

Everett opened the door, and Nora didn't fail to notice that his apartment was quiet. It didn't look like he had visitors, but she could be wrong. Besides, it wasn't any of her business.

When he caught her looking, she turned away and hurried outside.

# Chapter 3

Everett's magic required a lot of energy.

One time in university, he'd been so exhausted after making a large snow woman with big boobs—he blamed this on being a teenager—that he'd nearly passed out. He'd needed to wait an hour before walking home.

The key was to eat a lot beforehand. To eat until he was about to burst.

And so, for dinner tonight, Everett had gotten beef and broccoli, beef with black bean sauce, seafood chow mein, and wonton soup, all from a restaurant that he knew was generous with their portions. He ate every last bite—as well as half the chocolate in his extra advent calendar—then headed outside.

Before going to tonight's park, he went to a nearby house, where an older Chinese lady lived. He'd gotten to talking to her one day last winter when he'd helped with her groceries. After noticing that the previous day's snow was still on her driveway, he'd shoveled it and promised to take care of it from now on.

And he had. Sometimes he shoveled, but other times, like now, he used his ability to magically manipulate snow. It took him all of a minute, and once he was done, he got on the TTC and headed to tonight's park: Trinity Bellwoods.

At 10 p.m., this park was busier than the last one. He passed a group of teenagers doing who-knows-what and arrived at the spot he'd picked out years before. He could see the CN Tower in the distance.

Everett held up his mittened hands and moved them through the air, willing the snow to gather into a large pile. It was a bit like conducting an orchestra. Though it would take an awful lot of time to do this manually, with his powers he could create a sufficiently large pile in about ten minutes.

It truly was magical to watch as the snow appeared to defy gravity, as it swirled and sparkled under the light of the street lamps. While he was used to seeing snow move at his will, it hadn't lost its luster; he still enjoyed the experience. He had no idea if anyone else could move snow like this. If so, he'd never encountered them, and the thought made him feel rather lonely, but he quickly brushed it aside.

Once he'd gathered the snow, he pulled a folded sheet of paper out of his pocket and looked at his design. He had it memorized, but it was still comforting to have a look before he began the sculpting process.

He had to concentrate very hard to smooth the snow, to get those tusks just right, to make it look like the walrus was smiling. He'd once read an article about a similar sculpture, which had taken someone almost a hundred hours to create.

Everett, on the other hand, could do this in under two.

Finally, he finished the tail, and he stood back to admire his work. He snapped a picture before heading home.

·❤·❤·❤·❤·❤·

"Not again," Nora muttered as she sipped her morning coffee.

A "photo" of a large, smiling walrus made of snow was circulating on social media. Supposedly, it was in Trinity Bellwoods and had suddenly appeared overnight.

Why did someone want people to believe that snow sculptures were popping up across the city like magic?

She had no idea, but she looked at the comments to see if anyone else was calling out the lie. Sure enough, one of the top responses said it had to be generative AI.

But the top response to *that* was a picture of the walrus from a different angle. Someone had posted a photo of a woman touching one of the walrus's tusks. Another person had a video. There was additional photographic evidence of the hockey-playing bears, too.

Nora felt guilty that she'd dismissed the initial image as AI, but when so much stuff wasn't real, genuine things occasionally got caught in the fray. Why, someone probably thought her own writing was AI, although that could happen just because she loved em-dashes and the Oxford comma. Ugh.

People looked for any reason to dismiss something, and she was no exception, though her reasoning had certainly been better; she wouldn't write something off because of a legitimate punctuation mark.

As she finished her coffee and got to work, her mind kept drifting back to that walrus, and she decided she had to see it for herself. It would be a good way to enjoy—or, at least, attempt to enjoy—the Christmas season.

After finishing her work for the day, she put on her winter gear and headed to Trinity Bellwoods. She hadn't been to the park in years, and she wasn't sure she'd ever been in winter. Why would she have? She'd never lived in the area, and the last time she'd come, it had been to see the cherry blossoms.

Nora entered by the gates on Queen Street. Once upon a time, Trinity College had stood here. It had been demolished before she was born, but she'd seen black-and-white photos. It looked rather grand.

She'd been wandering through the park for several minutes, no walrus in sight, when she started wondering if maybe she'd been duped after all. She wasn't sure how—there had been multiple photos and videos from various accounts—but why couldn't she find it?

She took off her mittens and looked at her phone to see if anyone had posted information about the walrus's location. Sure enough, they had—it was closer to Dundas.

"Hi."

She looked up. A young man was standing in front of her, and he appeared to be with a young woman who was a few paces behind.

"Could I borrow your phone?" he asked. "Mine's dead. It's an emergency. Please."

Nora was instantly on alert. No way in hell was she giving a stranger her phone. She suspected this was a scam, and while she doubted things would get violent if she declined—there were lots of people around—she still stepped back before shaking her head.

"If you tell me the number," she said, her voice wavering slightly, "I can call and put it on speakerphone." Just in case he was telling the truth. She knew what it was like to have a family emergency, after all. "Or if it's not a phone call you need, you should be able to charge your phone at one of the coffee shops on Queen."

The man and woman simply turned away.

She blew out a breath. What had been their plan? She vaguely recalled hearing of a scam where someone asked to borrow your phone, then bolted. She swore she'd heard of others, too, but she couldn't recall the details now—she was too rattled.

Nora took several steps before realizing she was going in the wrong direction. After a few deep breaths, she reoriented herself and quickened her pace. She soon found a small crowd and saw a smiling walrus head rising above all the toques.

"Thank god," she muttered.

The sculpture was definitely real.

She stopped a couple of meters away and snapped some pictures.

"Hey, Nora."

In her surprise, she dropped her phone in the snow. She turned and saw Everett, dressed in a big red jacket. She exhaled slowly and picked up her phone.

"Sorry for scaring you." He gestured toward the giant walrus. "What do you think?"

It took her a moment to finish composing herself.

"It's impressive," she said. "Apparently, it just appeared overnight."

It was strange to encounter Everett somewhere other than the hallway of her building. Maybe that was why she found herself thinking he was rather cute, something that had never occurred to her before. It was a weird thing to think when she could see so little of his face. His hat was pulled down to his eyebrows, and his scarf was pulled up to his lips.

She shook her head, hoping to clear it of that thought, but it persisted.

She looked away from Everett and focused on the snow sculpture. On her trip down to the park, she'd seen some people arguing online about whether walruses could smile, of all things. But whether or not real walruses could smile, she liked that this one was doing so. It added to the whimsy of the sculpture.

And however it had been made, this snow walrus actually existed.

It was almost magical.

Nora felt a smile coming to her lips. Not quite as broad as the one on the snow walrus, but a smile nonetheless. Her wonder was amplified by all the people around her, everyone staring in amazement at the walrus.

"Can you take a picture of me?" Everett asked.

When she nodded, he handed over his phone, and she snapped a few pictures of him standing next to the walrus's right tusk. Then he moved out of the way so a little girl could take his place for photos. She wore a neon green snowsuit and was missing a front tooth.

"Want to see the other sculpture? It's a ten- or fifteen-minute walk from here, if you're up for it." Everett named the park.

Nora hadn't realized the other snow sculpture was so close, and she did want to see it, even if dusk was falling. The days were so short at this time of year. But she wasn't sure how enjoyable it would be to walk with Everett...and could she trust him? He wasn't a stranger, but she didn't know him well.

"All right," she said, wrapping her hand around the keys in her pocket, just in case.

She let him lead the way, and they traversed slushy streets toward the second sculpture. Everett didn't say much, but after they'd been walking for a few minutes, she felt herself relax. There was something comforting about the bulk of him next to her.

The second sculpture was smaller but more intricate than the first. It was also less crowded. There was one other couple taking photos, but otherwise—

Wait a second. Why was she thinking of them as a couple?

She wasn't. They were a couple of people standing together in a park, that was all, not an actual couple.

"What do you think?" Everett asked. "Which one do you like better?"

Maybe it was her imagination, but there was something odd about his voice. Like he really cared about her answer, and she couldn't understand why it would matter to him.

Yeah, it was probably her imagination.

Still, she considered the question seriously. "I'm not sure. They're both good, and they do look like they were made by the same person. Well, designed by the same person—multiple people might have been involved in the actual construction."

She could have sworn his lips twitched, but given the position of his scarf, it was hard to tell.

She pointed at one of the bears. "Do you play hockey?"

"No. I can skate, though not well."

"My sister played as a kid, but I was never interested."

Nora walked over to the bear and gently put her hand on its paw. It was nice to be able to touch it. She could see it was real with her own eyes, but still, the tactile confirmation was good. She was careful not to ruin anything; she wanted other people to be able to enjoy the bear. It had been sculpted a few days ago, and it was covered in the light dusting of snow that had fallen since then.

She and Everett walked away from the park together.

"You heading back to the apartment?" she asked.

"No, I'm going to have ice cream."

"In this weather?" As far as winter days went, it wasn't the worst, but it definitely wasn't ice cream weather. She shivered just at the thought.

"It's near Ossington Station." He inclined his head to the north. "I'll eat the ice cream indoors, of course."

Still, it didn't sound appealing to her.

"It's a bakery," he said. "They have other things to eat, plus hot chocolate and tea, if that's more your speed. I mean, if you're interested," he added. "Not that you need to be."

Hm. Drinking hot chocolate with him was tempting. Not that he, himself, was tempting, but the promise of a hot beverage sounded nice. And if it was near the subway station...

"Sure, why not," she said.

# Chapter 4

IT WAS A BIT of a walk to the bakery. Nora stayed silent at first, but Everett apparently felt the need to make conversation.

"Have you lived in Toronto long?" he asked.

"Yeah, a long time," she replied.

"Did you grow up here?"

"Burlington." It wasn't all that far away. Well, it could be if traffic was shit, which it usually was. But she had no reason to go to Burlington anymore, so it didn't matter. "You?"

"The Bay Area," he said, "then Victoria."

"The winter here must have been quite a shock to you after that."

She wondered what it would be like to live in a place like San Francisco, which didn't have seasons in the same way as Toronto. Even though she hated winter, would she miss it?

Maybe she would.

It occurred to Nora that it had been a long time since she'd had a getting-to-know-you conversation. It might have happened more often if she did things like date, but she didn't. Her small family and Aimee were the important people in her life, and she rarely spoke to anyone else. Normally, she told herself that was fine and she didn't miss socializing, but this was kind of nice.

"What do you do?" she asked. "For work, I mean."

"IT support."

That sounded like a nightmare. Mind you, an awful lot of jobs sounded nightmarish to her. But the idea of dealing with people who did ass-backward things to their machines—or couldn't perform basic troubleshooting—sounded horrific. Though to be fair, she probably didn't have an accurate idea of what his typical day was like.

They arrived at the small bakery, and Nora could see why Everett liked it. Anyone who liked the Christmas season would appreciate a place that was festooned with a variety of garlands and painted gingerbread men, each wearing a Santa hat.

And the ice cream? They'd gone all out with the Christmas flavors. There was eggnog (gross), candy cane (slightly more palatable), roasted chestnut, and gingerbread house. Not gingerbread, but gingerbread house: swirled in with the ice cream were broken pieces of assorted candy. Could you put a whole gingerbread house into an ice cream maker? That's what appeared to have happened.

Nora selected her plain hot chocolate—she avoided any of their special seasonal offerings—and Everett got a cup of gingerbread house ice cream. In silent agreement, they headed to a table at the very back. That way, she wouldn't be chilled by cold air whenever someone opened the door.

Everett took off his jacket and scarf, but not his toque. He was wearing a wool sweater that looked particularly cozy. As he started eating his ice cream, she found herself thinking that there was something incongruous about that tiny spoon in his large hand.

"Good?" she asked.

"Very." He crunched a mint.

She'd take his word for it.

"You wouldn't order this for yourself?" he said.

"Well..."

"Ah, I know." He held up a finger as he had another small bite of ice cream. "Not enough gumdrops." His voice was solemn.

A giggle escaped her lips. An actual *giggle*.

Everett's serious expression turned into a smile.

"Yes," she said, "not enough black gumdrops."

"You like the licorice ones? Gross."

"Have you ever made a gingerbread house?" She was pretty sure of the answer, but she asked anyway.

"I have, but only from a kit."

She couldn't recall the last time she'd been gently teased by a man. Her brother-in-law was the only man she saw on a semi-regular basis, and he wasn't the teasing sort. Back in university, she'd briefly dated a guy whose teasing was downright mean.

She couldn't imagine Everett being mean, but she reminded herself that she still didn't know him very well, and even people you thought you knew could surprise you. Besides, she'd proven herself to be a rather poor judge of character.

"Is something wrong?" Everett asked.

"Just thinking about all the stuff I have to do tonight," she lied.

He nodded and returned his attention to his treat. A droplet of melted ice cream clung to his beard, and she itched to wipe it away.

In an attempt to rid herself of that urge, she dove into her hot chocolate. Some hot chocolate was more sugary than chocolatey, but this stuff didn't have that problem. No, it was very, very good. Rich and luxurious.

"Does it meet your approval?" he asked.

"It does, and you know I have very fine tastes. Your palate just isn't sophisticated enough for black gumdrops."

Though privately, she agreed with him: licorice-flavored gumdrops were disgusting. But the purpose of her comment had been to make him smile, and it worked. Though why she cared about that, she wasn't sure.

She had another sip of her drink. The hot chocolate warmed her from the inside. She had a good winter jacket, but she still got cold when she spent an hour or more outside in the winter.

Yes, this hit the spot.

"I know it's not your favorite time of year," Everett said, "but do you have any plans for Christmas?"

She shook her head. "Not on the twenty-fifth—or anytime around then. I'm celebrating on Saturday with my sister and her family."

"What does that entail?"

"Going to her house in Mississauga, opening gifts with my niece and nephew, and eating ham."

Their mother had always preferred doing a ham over a turkey. Easier, she said. It was a tradition they'd continued without her.

"They're going away later in the month," she explained, "so I can't see them then. What about you?"

"I usually visit my family out west," he said, "but I'm not going this year."

"Yeah, that's a long way, and it must be a pain to fly during the holidays."

Flying wasn't her idea of a good time in general, but in December, when there was a chance that a snowstorm could derail your plans? That definitely didn't sound fun. If she had to spend twenty-four hours in an airport at Christmas, she'd probably end up stabbing someone with an icicle decoration, or hitting them over the head with an overpriced sandwich. She'd nearly done something similar at her retail job last December—she'd needed to work two holiday seasons to earn back the money she'd given to Samuel. Although she tried not to worry too much about the security of her full-time job, she did her best to maintain a healthy savings account.

"But I'm sorry you can't see your family," she added.

Or maybe Everett wasn't going to see his family because they had a strained relationship. She shouldn't assume that he'd want to see them.

"It's fine," he said. "I'm going for Lunar New Year instead."

In the silence that followed, Nora was very *aware*. Aware that they were both single—or, at least, unmarried—people who were not seeing their families for the holidays. It was a ridiculous thought, but she felt like she should offer to celebrate with him, just in case he didn't have any plans for December 25.

She was also very aware that this was quite a small table. She shifted in her chair, her knee bumping against his. A little hot chocolate spilled over the rim of her cup, and she nearly wept. It seemed a crime to waste any of it. She wiped the table with a napkin.

Once she finished her drink, she stood up, and Everett followed her. They disposed of their garbage and headed back into the cold.

After saying goodbye to Everett and stepping into her apartment, Nora changed into some more comfortable clothes. She made herself a cup of tea as she texted pictures of the snow sculptures to her sister. There was a pleasant warmth in her chest, a warmth that didn't come from drinking hot beverages on cold days but something different.

She wouldn't examine that too closely.

But hanging out with Everett had been easy. More comfortable than it should have been. Not once had she gotten the sense that he wanted anything out of her. It didn't seem like he was trying to con her or charm her or sleep with her.

That shouldn't feel like a novelty, but it was, and it had been just what she needed after the possible scam attempt earlier. If she hadn't run into him, she might have spent more time obsessing over it.

She didn't mention Everett in her texts to her sister. Brianna would have taken it the wrong way—assumed it had been a date—so it was better not to say anything at all. Her sister didn't reply right away, but that was okay. She was probably trying to wrangle two small children into bed.

Too lazy to move from the couch, Nora scrolled through social media as she drank her tea. She came across two headlines that she assumed were satire but turned out to be real, someone recommending fresh air to cure depression and cancer, and a bunch of men absolutely losing it on a woman who said she wouldn't marry anyone who refused to eat leftovers. Then she saw some disturbingly incorrect information about vaccines.

Hm. Maybe she shouldn't spend her free time online.

She also came across a recipe for gumdrop cake, which she wanted to send to Everett, except she didn't know his number.

Ah well.

She heated up leftovers for dinner (she was definitely #teamleftovers), did a few chores, and watched a show.

Nothing unusual, although she was eating a bit later than usual thanks to her earlier excursion.

When she climbed into bed, she couldn't help wishing there was somebody next to her under the covers, and that somebody looked like...

No one in particular.

Nope, she certainly didn't have anyone on her mind.

Her thoughts turned to the snow sculptures. Hopefully, the weather would remain cold enough so the snow didn't melt, and hopefully, there would be a third one soon.

# Chapter 5

WHILE EATING HER LUNCH on Friday, Nora came across an article about the snow sculptures.

*Toronto Enthralled by Mysterious Sculptures*

Apparently, a third one had appeared overnight, in a park close to where she lived. She scrolled to the picture: a hippo wearing a Santa hat and holding a bag of toys.

She might not be a Christmas person, but like the other sculptures, it made her smile.

Nobody knew who was making the sculptures or how they managed to pull them off so quickly. Based on the locations of the first two sculptures, a few people had camped out at a nearby park in the west end, thinking it might be next and hoping to figure out who was behind it all. But they'd been wrong about the location, and no one had seen anything at the latest park.

Nora couldn't imagine being that dedicated to such a mystery.

She continued reading the article. The author had interviewed a snow sculpture expert—how did one become an expert in such things?—who made it sound like it was impossible for one or two people to do it all in a single night. He was mystified by the sculptures, but he admired the skill it had taken to make them.

Yes, it had to be a coordinated effort, and presumably, whoever was behind these would want credit at some point, but until then, Nora would simply enjoy them. There weren't enough things to enjoy in this hellscape of a world, and so she'd do what she could.

Perhaps, after she finished work for the day, she'd go to see this one in person.

## City Captivated by Snow Banksy

Snow Banksy! Ha!

Everett couldn't help the burst of laughter that escaped his lips. His stunt was capturing people's fancy just liked he'd hoped it would.

Then, of course, he had to ruin his good mood by reading a diatribe from someone who thought it was stupid and represented everything that was wrong with Toronto.

To cheer himself up, he put aside his phone and recalled when he'd come across Nora at Trinity Bellwoods. He'd made the trip down because he wanted to see people's reactions in person. His neighbor might scoff at snow angels and sleigh rides, but she'd gone to see his sculptures, and if nothing else, the delight on her face had been worth it.

And then he'd watched her drink hot chocolate. She hadn't asked the barista to hold the whipped cream, as he'd thought she might do; no, she'd licked the foamy peak and gotten a little on her lower lip.

It was fun to watch Nora indulge herself. He had the sense that it wasn't a common occurrence, even if she claimed she didn't need the excuse of Christmas to enjoy sweets. Sure, she might not have eaten gingerbread ice cream loaded with chocolate and pretzel bits and other things, but Everett could appreciate that it wasn't for everyone.

He wanted to know everything she liked.

Just before four o'clock, he knocked on her door and hoped he wasn't being too presumptuous. She answered half a minute later, wearing yoga pants and a hoodie. Her light brown hair was loose around her shoulders.

"If you're finished work for the day," he said, "would you like to see the latest sculpture together?" He, on the other hand, hadn't done any work—it was one of the days he'd scheduled off so he could conduct his plan without running himself ragged. "But if you don't—"

"No, no, that sounds good. I was thinking of going anyway. Give me another twenty minutes to finish up, and I'll meet you in the hall."

Twenty minutes later, she emerged from her apartment. He refrained from saying she looked cute in that knit hat with its white pompom, but she did. *Very* cute.

"Where did your wreath go?" She gestured to his door.

"It's against the Ontario Fire Code, apparently."

"I'm sorry," she said.

He bowed his head in a moment of silence for his poor wreath. "Are you ready to head out? Looks like it's a fifteen-minute walk."

It had been nice to make a snow sculpture nearby; he hadn't needed to get on the TTC afterward. But on the way home, he'd been so tired that the trip had taken him twenty-three minutes.

They set out into the cold, and Nora walked at a brisk pace. Did she walk this fast in the summer, or was it only to keep warm in the winter?

When they arrived at the sculpture, there were several people standing around it. A small group of teenagers, all wearing clothes that didn't look warm enough for the weather. A few young children. A baby in a blue hat with ears, securely held by an older relative. A middle-aged couple.

"Dada, it's a hippo!" shouted a little boy.

Everett was glad he'd come. Seeing the reaction online wasn't quite the same.

But for whatever reason, observing Nora's response was the best part. He tried not to stare at her slow smile of wonder. He didn't need to see the sculpture himself—he knew all the details intimately—but he turned to look at it anyway so he didn't appear suspicious. Though it wasn't like she'd suspect the truth.

"If I had to choose a favorite animal," she said, "it would be the hippo."

"Yeah?" he said. "Why's that?"

"Because they're mean. Not that I, personally, have come across a hippo in the wild, but they seem like they don't take shit from anyone. They're vicious."

"Do you feel a kinship with them?" He tried to make his tone light. Teasing.

She rewarded him with another smile, this one rather different from the last. It was a smile that spoke of mischief, rather than delight or wonder, and he forgot to breathe.

"I do," she replied at last.

"Should I be worried?" This time he knew he didn't succeed in making his tone light. There was something about the way the fading light danced on her pink cheeks... it made him uncharacteristically serious. She was breathtaking. He wished he could capture her expression in a sketch or a snow sculpture, but he knew he wouldn't be able to do it justice.

He also wished he could cup her cheeks and warm them.

When she took a tiny step closer to him, he couldn't help wondering if she felt the same way. If she wanted to kiss him in the cold, among the small crowd of people who'd gathered to admire a snow hippo.

But she didn't. She just said, "I think you're okay. For now."

And then he realized that she'd stepped closer to him because there was a family right behind her. It was silly to have thought she might want to kiss him.

"So," Nora said, "what do you think is the story behind the sculptures?"

He shrugged. "It's got to be...a well-organized group of people. They must have everything carefully planned in advance."

She nodded. "Why do you think they're doing it?"

"For fun?"

"Hanging out in the snow for hours at night isn't my idea of fun, but I suppose it could be for some people."

"Because they want to spread Christmas cheer?"

She rolled her eyes. "Maybe. I wonder if it's meant to entertain the city at large—or if it's mainly for someone in particular."

He didn't, of course, say that when he'd made this sculpture, he'd thought of her more than anyone else.

Well, most of the time, he'd been concentrating on the snow. But when his thoughts wandered for a second or two, it was mostly to her.

"Their children, perhaps," he said instead.

"Yeah. Maybe they're claiming Santa was responsible."

"Did you ever believe in Santa?"

"Until I was six, but I pretended for longer."

"Why?" he asked.

"Because of my younger sister. Also, I was afraid that if I told my mom, she'd stop giving me presents from Santa, and then I'd get fewer gifts at Christmas."

"Ah, you were being practical."

"I was a mercenary child, yes." She shook her head. "I should have known my mother wouldn't do that to me. I got presents from Santa even in university."

There was a wistful look on her face, and he understood, without her saying the words, that her mother was gone. He knew she wouldn't want him to mention it, not now, and he couldn't help wondering if the loss had affected her feelings toward Christmas.

She turned back to the sculpture and took a few pictures. Then she rubbed her hands together and put on her mittens.

"Let's go," she said.

They were five minutes from their apartment building when Nora stopped in front of a shawarma restaurant.

"I'm going to grab something to eat," she said. "I don't feel like cooking tonight. You don't need to join me, but you can if you'd like."

He joined her.

Once they had their sandwiches, they sat at the counter by the window. His ass was a little too big for the stool, and while it seemed sturdy, it wasn't the most comfortable. But that was okay. It wouldn't take long to eat. And there were other reasons, too, that he didn't mind.

"You're doing Christmas with your sister this weekend?" he said.

She nodded. "What are your plans? More holiday decorating?"

"No, I've got some errands to run."

He hadn't thought it would bother him that he couldn't tell anyone the truth about the sculptures. He'd discovered his magic more than twenty years ago; he was used to this. But now, something in him ached to reveal it. To her.

"Sounds exciting." She reached for a piece of cucumber that was threatening to escape from her sandwich. "Do you think there will be more sculptures?"

"I do," he said, "but not tonight."

"They've been three days apart so far. Presumably, Sunday night will be next?"

"That seems reasonable." He swallowed. "Would you...would you like to see the next one together, if it works out?"

She didn't grace him with one of her smiles, but she did say, "I would."

It caused a flutter in his chest.

# Chapter 6

"Are you sure you don't want to come home for Christmas?" his mother asked. "There are still flights. I checked earlier and—"

"I'm sure." Everett sank down heavily on his couch. He was trying to conserve his energy for tonight, but talking to his parents wasn't always relaxing. "I'll be there in February, remember?"

"Is it a financial issue? Because—"

"It's not. Don't worry, Ma."

She huffed. "You know that's impossible."

He could hear the smile in her voice.

"I read in the paper," she said, "that mysterious snow sculptures have appeared in Toronto."

Huh. He hadn't thought that his mother, out in B.C., would hear about this, though he supposed she paid attention to Toronto news because he lived here.

"Yes," he said. "I went to see one yesterday because it's, um, close to my apartment."

"There was a picture of one sculpture. A hippo." She clicked her tongue. "It was impressive, but I don't know why anyone would put a Santa hat on a hippo. They live nowhere near the North Pole!"

He smothered a laugh and refrained from defending his artistic choices.

After ending the call, Everett debated what food to gorge himself on tonight. Before he could decide, he received a text from a friend, asking if he'd like to watch the Leafs game at a bar. He wished he could—he hadn't seen this friend in a couple of months—but he didn't want to change his plans.

He made an excuse about feeling a little under the weather and suggested they meet up another time. Then he ordered two large pizzas with pepperoni and mushrooms. He'd leave a couple of slices for a middle-of-the-night snack when he returned home.

At ten o'clock, he ate some star-shaped shortbread cookies, put on his winter gear, and locked his apartment. He glanced at Nora's door and wondered if she was back from celebrating Christmas with her sister. He hadn't heard her return, but depending on where he was in his apartment, he didn't always hear noise in the hallway.

He hoped she had a good time.

He also hoped she enjoyed the next sculpture. It was slightly more involved than the last one, and it would probably take him three hours. He'd planned it out ages ago, but now, because of what the snow animals in question would be doing, he couldn't help but think of her.

With her company, he'd felt less alone lately.

"Welcome to your new home," Nora said.

She couldn't believe she was talking to a plush green dinosaur. She wasn't quite sure which kind of dinosaur he was supposed to be. If she had to guess, she'd say a T-Rex, but he was certainly the least threatening T-Rex in existence.

It had been a Christmas gift from her three-year-old nephew, who'd ruined the surprise within thirty seconds of her arrival. When she'd finally unwrapped the gift, he'd proclaimed that the dinosaur was named Dino, and he'd made her promise to talk to Dino and tuck him into bed each night. She didn't intend to speak to him every night, but she could at least do it once. It would feel wrong to break a promise to a small child.

Her phone vibrated on her bedside table. It was Aimee, saying that she'd decided to go home with the man she'd met on an app—it was their second time meeting up in person. She provided an address.

Nora told her friend to have a good time, then set her phone to Do Not Disturb, with Aimee's number as an exception. She turned out the light and settled under the covers.

But for some reason, she couldn't sleep. Maybe it was thanks to all the ham and chocolate she'd consumed earlier, or her concern about Aimee.

Or because she wasn't used to sharing her bed.

A plush dinosaur on the other side of her queen bed shouldn't disrupt her sleep. He was, after all, very small—and he didn't snore or steal the blankets. At least, he hadn't done so yet.

But he was the only thing that was different about her sleeping environment.

At one thirty in the morning, Nora took Dino to her couch, murmuring apologies as she settled him against a throw pillow. Then she returned to bed.

She'd rarely had trouble falling asleep when she was younger, but the older she got, the more frequently she was plagued by insomnia. By the time she turned seventy, she'd probably stop sleeping altogether.

If there was still a world to sleep in, that was. Occasionally, she had her doubts.

After tossing and turning for another hour, she gave up on getting some shuteye, grabbed her phone, and went to join Dino on the couch.

"Sorry," she said as she accidentally shoved him onto the carpet. She picked him up and was about to set him on the coffee table when she changed her mind. Maybe cuddling a plushie would calm her brain. It seemed unlikely, but at this point, she was willing to try anything.

She was definitely losing it.

With Dino safely snuggled against her chest, she settled on the couch and opened the Sudoku app on her phone. This would be better for her state of mind than, say, going on social media and stumbling across posts that referred to a novel set in the nineties as historical fiction. Or, worse, people who supported book banning.

She'd just finished an easy puzzle when she heard someone walking down the hallway. The footsteps stopped near her door, and she froze.

It was probably Everett, coming home late after a night out. She wouldn't have pegged him as the sort to be out until almost three in the morning, but what did she know?

Still, even though it was most likely her neighbor, her body tensed, as if on high alert.

There was a loud thud.

Nora walked to the door. Not sure what she'd find, she opened it slowly. Cautiously.

Everett was lying on the floor.

# Chapter 7

"ARE YOU OKAY?" NORA asked, then felt ridiculous.

Everett obviously wasn't okay. He was lying face-down in the hallway, one arm cushioning his head, the rest of his limbs splayed. He wore his usual winter jacket and hat, and something in her twisted. Her mind flashed back to three years ago, when mother had collapsed. They'd spent their last Christmas together in the hospital. Since Brianna had had a baby and a toddler at home, much of the care had fallen to Nora.

His eyelids fluttered. "Um...ugh..."

At least he was conscious.

"Don't worry." She tried to sound calm, tried not to show the panic she still felt. "I'm calling an ambulance. You—"

"No. Don't need...ambulance." His voice was weak.

"Are you drunk?"

"No." He struggled to sit. He was sweaty and pale.

"Do you know what happened?"

He nodded, though he didn't provide any details. "Need…food."

He started to get up, but his legs didn't seem strong enough.

"Hand me your keys," she said.

When he passed them over, she opened the door and dragged him inside. It was no small feat, as he weighed a lot more than she did.

Finally, she had him settled against the door. She went to the fridge and found a container with two slices of pizza. She didn't bother to warm them up; she took the container right to him.

"This okay?" she asked, sitting down on the floor next to him.

In response, he picked up a piece and took a bite.

"Mis…calculated," he said. "Wanted to make it…extra nice…for you."

Nora had no idea what he was talking about. Or maybe he had no idea who she was.

She decided not to clarify what he meant.

She still didn't know what was wrong, and she wouldn't ask. He didn't owe her any medical information, but whatever this was, it seemed like it had happened before, and after half a slice of pizza, he did look better. She hoped it was nothing serious, yet she kept thinking of the worst-case scenarios.

"Water?" she asked.

When he nodded, she stood up again. She quickly located a water bottle next to the advent calendar in the kitchen, and she brought it back to him.

"Thank...you."

She had the sudden urge to run her hand through his hair, to comfort him with her touch. But they didn't have that sort of relationship, and so she kept her hands to herself.

She also wanted to tell him that she'd appreciated his company lately—it was helping her get through a difficult season, full of bad memories. But she didn't say that, either.

"You can go," he said. "Okay now."

"No, not yet. A few more minutes."

He didn't argue, just finished the second slice of pizza in a few bites before guzzling half the bottle of water.

"Do you need anything else to eat?" she asked.

"Granola bar. Above the sink."

She had to stand on her toes to reach the shelf. She brought the whole box, just in case.

"Help yourself," he said as he opened one up. Despite his condition, he was still trying to be a decent host.

She shook her head.

The left corner of his mouth hitched up. "Maybe your friend...would like one."

This was when Nora realized, in horror, that Dino was tucked under her armpit.

"A Christmas present from my nephew," she said.

"Sure it was."

She glared at him.

"How was your early Christmas celebration?" he asked.

He was rapidly improving, his voice much clearer than it had been five minutes ago. She'd feel comfortable enough to leave him soon. Still...

"You just passed out in the hallway," she said. "We're talking about you. Not me."

"Hm." That was his only response before he returned to crunching on the granola bar. He brushed a crumb from his beard before his gaze dropped down. Was he looking at her hippo pajama pants? She couldn't help wishing she'd worn her plaid ones, but how the hell could she have known that she'd see anyone tonight?

Nora was suddenly conscious of her gray waffle shirt—her nipples were probably visible. She wished she didn't care about that, but she did. She crossed her arms over her chest, which squished Dino against her breast.

But that wasn't important right now; what mattered was making sure Everett was safe.

"Can you stand up?" she asked.

When he nodded, she got up and offered him a hand. He took it, his large hand engulfing hers, and staggered to his feet. He managed to remove his jacket and boots.

"I'm going to go," she said. "But if you need anything...here, let me put my number in your phone. You can text me."

He handed over his phone, and the left side of his mouth curved up again. "You're giving me your number? You must—"

"Shut it." She placed a finger to his lips.

The softness and warmth of his lips caught her off guard. She immediately withdrew and curled her fingers into a fist so they wouldn't tingle.

Was there anything else she should tell him? Her mind was suddenly blank.

Ah. Right.

"Text me when you wake up," she said. "Let me know you're okay."

"Will do."

She gave him one last look before heading back across the hall, Dino in her arms. Although she didn't expect to fall asleep right away, sleep pulled her under almost as soon as her head hit the pillow.

Everett opened his eyes. His bedroom was unusually bright, and he glanced at his alarm clock.

1:05 p.m.

Holy crap. He couldn't remember the last time he'd slept in so much.

He was lying on top of his quilt, and he was still wearing his jeans and sweater. As he sat up, the events of last night slowly returned to him.

He'd gone to a park in the east end, as planned, and made the sculpture. It had taken him a long time, and he'd barely managed to catch the last subway train. His head had pounded the whole ride home, a sign he'd overexerted himself. He'd drunk the juice and eaten the trail mix he'd brought with him, but even with all the pizza he'd consumed earlier, it hadn't been enough. He'd told himself he was okay, he just had to make it home. It was only ten minutes, if that, from the station.

But the short walk had taken a lot out of him, and he'd collapsed by his door.

Everett typically tried to be very careful, to make sure he had enough energy for the magic he intended to conduct. He hadn't had any incidents in years...until last night, when Nora had found him in the hallway.

How embarrassing.

His memory of what happened next was a little foggy, but he vaguely remembered eating pizza while sitting on the floor, and he remembered her concern. The furrow between her brows. The fuzzy dinosaur under her arm. The way she entered her number into his phone and made him promise to text when he woke up.

Her bossiness had been rather hot.

That should have been the furthest thing from his mind ten minutes after collapsing, but he remembered thinking it. He also recalled how her finger had felt against his lips. When she'd snatched her finger back, much to his disappointment, the feeling had lingered.

Not wanting her to worry, he pulled out his phone.

> **Everett:** Just got up. Thank you for looking after me last night.

Her reply came not thirty seconds later.

> **Nora:** How are you feeling?

> **Everett:** I'm doing fine

He couldn't tell her what had been wrong, but he could say that much. He really was fine now, aside from the fact that he's slept on his shoulder funny. But he was well rested, and as soon as he had a shower, he'd feel refreshed.

**Nora:** There's another snow sculpture. I know we talked about seeing it together, but if you're not well enough, I understand.

**Everett:** No, I'm up for it. How's two thirty?

·❤·❤·❤·❤·❤·

Nora met him in the hallway. Unlike last night, she wasn't accompanied by a plush dinosaur.

She looked him up and down with an assessing gaze. Everett wished she were checking him out, but he knew she was trying to evaluate his health.

"Are you sure you can handle it?" she asked.

"I'm sure."

She tapped her cross-body bag. "I've got food and water in here if you need it."

He was touched that she was looking out for him. He'd brought some trail mix too, just in case, though he didn't expect any problems.

When he'd first met Nora—a week or two after he moved in, if he remembered correctly—they exchanged only a few words. Enough for him to get the impression that she was rather aloof. And that was fine.

But in the past week or so, he'd seen a different side of her, and now, he wanted to spend more and more time in her presence.

"How was your Christmas celebration?" he asked as they stepped into the elevator.

She gave him an odd look.

"Oh, did I ask that last night?" He frowned. "I don't remember your answer, sorry."

"Because I didn't answer. Anyway, it was good."

"There wasn't too much Christmas music and cheer for you?"

"Well, there were some very creative lyrics to the tune of 'Jingle Bells.'"

"The Batman ones?"

"Slightly different from any Batman lyrics I'd heard before, though it was hard to tell. Even though they sang it at least a dozen times, there was too much laughter to make out all the words."

He smiled at the image. "How old are the kids?"

"My niece is five and my nephew is three. My sister's kids."

"This is the nephew who gave you the dinosaur?"

"I was hoping you'd forget about that," she muttered.

"I didn't. In fact, I got your dino a little gift." Just something he'd found it in his closet.

"How disturbing."

"Please hold your judgment until you see it."

"I'll try," she huffed, but her lips twitched.

It took them more than forty-five minutes to get to the latest sculpture, owing to a mechanical issue on the TTC. All the other times they'd gone to see the snow sculptures, it had been dusk, but now, the sun shone brightly and it was difficult to get a good look at the sculpture because of the large crowd.

"Dammit, I'm too short," Nora said.

"I could carry you."

"Ha."

He'd been joking, but had she wanted, he would have acquiesced.

When a group moved aside, he and Nora took their place, and she had no trouble seeing past the small children in front of her.

"I didn't think there would be one today," she said. "The others were three days apart, so I figured it would be tomorrow."

"Maybe they're trying to be unpredictable."

In her subsequent silence, he couldn't help wondering if she had any suspicions about him—he'd come home late last night, and the next morning, a snow sculpture had appeared—but she gave no indication of it.

"What do you think?" he asked, gesturing to the two rabbits and their mugs of hot chocolate. The rabbits were sitting by a fireplace.

"I just can't believe this was all done in one night, and nobody saw it happening. In this day and age, there's always someone with a phone around."

"Yeah, it does seem unlikely."

"Yet it's here. The sculptures are real, and that's what I care about. In a world where people are always trying to get you to believe things that aren't true... they're *real*."

She spoke the last part with such conviction, and it sent a chill down his spine.

Or maybe that was the gust of wind.

"A bit of Christmas magic," he murmured. It was truer than she could know.

She took a few pictures, and then they walked back to the subway. On the way, she absently picked up some snow and made a snowball with her mittened hands. She threw it at the trunk of a tree.

Back in their apartment building, outside their respective doors, he hesitated after putting his key in the lock. "Nora," he said, his voice weirdly scratchy, "would you like to come in? For hot chocolate or hot buttered rum?" He paused. "As a thank you for last night."

As he waited for her response, his heart thumped wildly.

She didn't smile, but she did give him the answer he'd hoped to hear.

"Yes."

# Chapter 8

Before going to Everett's, Nora went to her apartment to strip off her winter clothes. On one hand, she wished he hadn't added "as a thank you for last night." It made the invitation feel a bit transactional, and she'd prefer that he simply want to see her.

"What's wrong with me?" she muttered as she hung up her winter jacket.

But on the other hand, there had been something touching about the uncertainty in his voice—he was worried about making her uncomfortable.

She wasn't used to these feelings. She didn't appreciate them. It felt like this was evolving into more than a casual friendship to help her survive the Christmas season, to ease the knot of loneliness in her chest.

But despite her misgivings, she put on a pair of flip-flops and headed across the hallway. Everett opened the door. He didn't look like a man who'd collapsed less than twenty-four hours ago. Whatever had happened, he'd recovered quite well. The memories of her mother's frailty, those nights spent in a hospital chair, seemed further away than they had last night.

"It's been a while," he said, and despite herself, she laughed.

There was just something endearing about Everett. That flannel shirt and those square frames and the ever-present smile. While she'd never had a thing for beards before, on him, she rather liked it.

*What's wrong with me?*

This time, she didn't say it out loud. At least, she hoped the words didn't come out of her mouth but stayed in her brain.

She really wasn't used to feeling this way around a man. She hadn't been the least bit tempted by anyone in ages—and that had ended horribly.

No, she was a sensible, skeptical forty-year-old woman...who was, for some reason, experiencing the slightest flutter in her chest.

Maybe that was why she said something completely nonsensical.

"You said you had a gift for Dino."

"So I did. But he's not here to receive it."

"You want me to go and get him?" she asked.

"Or I can give him the gift at a later date."

Despite her better judgment, Nora went to grab the plush dinosaur from her apartment. She couldn't believe she was doing this, but she was the tiniest bit curious about what the gift could be, and perhaps she was also a little envious of Dino—

No! What was wrong with her?

She returned with the dinosaur in hand, and Everett held up a thick red ribbon.

"You're going to Christmas-fy my dinosaur?" she asked.

"He wants to get in the Christmas spirit."

She didn't protest and say that her dinosaur didn't celebrate the holiday; no, she handed him over and allowed Everett to tie the ribbon in a bow around Dino's chubby neck. She supposed her nephew would appreciate the pictures.

Everett handed back the dinosaur, his fingers accidentally—she assumed—brushing hers. Not wanting to hold on to Dino as she had last night, she set him on the coffee table.

"So," he said, "hot chocolate? Spiked hot chocolate? Hot buttered rum? Tea?"

"Hot buttered rum, but go easy on the rum. I'm working tomorrow."

She sat down on the couch as he headed to the kitchen and turned on the kettle. There was a small artificial Christmas tree on the end table next to her. She rolled her eyes, but to her distress, it was a rather fond eye roll.

Needing a distraction from the Christmas spirit in Everett's apartment, she pulled out her phone. Apparently, she had an overdue 407 bill. Ha! That was a lie.

And in other news, the first snow sculpture had been destroyed.

When Everett returned with two mugs—both had reindeer on them—she turned her phone toward him. He blinked as he set the mugs down on coasters. "It's...gone?"

It was rather cute to see this large man upset over a snow sculpture, but his troubled look also heightened the pang she felt. Something that had brought them a scrap of joy was no longer there.

"Yes," she said. "It's good we went to see it when we did."

He nodded. "At least...a lot of people got to see it. It was there for over a week."

"It would suck to be one of the people who made the sculpture. To have your hard work destroyed. Of course, it would have melted eventually—it was never meant to be permanent—but still."

She supposed that was part of the magic: like cherry blossoms in the spring, a snow sculpture couldn't last. In Toronto, it wasn't uncommon for the temperature to get above freezing in the winter, but this December had been colder than usual.

"Yes," he said, "it would."

She couldn't help thinking of completed movies that never saw the light day because they were written off for tax purposes. It was revolting. Millions upon millions of dollars could be spent, and people could dedicate years to a project that wouldn't be released to the public—a decision that might have absolutely nothing to do with the movie's quality. And you never knew what might disappear from streaming services. Nora tried to buy physical versions of anything she loved, just in case.

There was so much wrong in this world, but for now, she was here with her neighbor. She picked up a mug. It warmed her hands, and she inhaled deeply. There was a touch of cinnamon and other spices.

"I've never had hot buttered rum before," she said.

He sat down next to her, but he was careful not to get too close. "I first had it at a Christmas-themed pop-up bar a couple of years ago."

She'd never understood the appeal of such bars. Why would she want to squeeze into a crowded room and take pictures with a blow-up Santa Claus or similar, while sipping an expensive drink decorated with too much cheer?

Yet she was in a room with too much Christmas cheer right now, a hot boozy drink in her hand, and she didn't mind. She supposed it helped that she'd only had to walk across the hall—and there was only one other person here.

Nora took a sip of her drink and almost groaned. It was wonderfully warm and rich, perfect after spending time outside. There was a bite of alcohol, but it wasn't too strong.

She turned toward Everett. "That's really good."

"I make a big batch of...well, it's a batter of sorts, with butter and brown sugar and...other things. I keep it in the freezer..."

He was having trouble getting words out, like he had in the middle of the night—but it was different this time. It seemed that his gaze was fixated on her mouth. Experimentally, she licked her upper lip, and he tracked the movement.

His apartment suddenly felt a lot smaller than it was.

It had been a long time since anyone had looked at Nora this way. On one hand, it caused an unconscious thrill in her body. Some of the thoughts and feelings she had...they seemed to be reciprocated.

On the other hand, she couldn't help but be reminded of what had happened last time, and she didn't trust her ability to figure out what was genuine and what was not. She'd been foolish, so foolish. And while it was a little different, she'd thought the original picture of the now-demolished snow sculpture was fake, and she'd been wrong. How could she be confident in her own judgment?

Everett leaned closer. She didn't move; she felt like she was balanced on a tiny point, and if she shifted in any direction, she'd tip over.

He stood up abruptly, some of his drink sloshing over the side of his mug.

She shouldn't be so disappointed.

"Crap," he said as he bustled to the kitchen. He returned with a poinsettia-patterned towel and cleaned up the small spill. "I'm sorry."

"Why are you saying sorry?" she asked. "It's *your* floor."

He sat down on the recliner rather than on the couch. "The way I was looking at you...I thought...but I was wrong."

*Oh.* He'd moved because he'd figured she wasn't interested.

He scrubbed a hand over his face. "If you want to leave, I understand."

She couldn't seem to form any words; she wasn't even sure what she wanted to say.

But she knew what she wanted to do, and while a voice at the back of her head was telling her that this wasn't a great idea, it seemed very far away now. Couldn't she just take what she wanted? Surely, giving in to this one small impulse wouldn't lead to disaster.

She took a bracing sip of hot buttered rum before setting down the half-empty mug and walking toward the recliner. She didn't let herself meet Everett's gaze until she got there, and when she did...

He was looking at her with confusion and hope.

"You weren't wrong," she said, at last able to speak. "Put down your drink."

Once he did, she sat on his lap and straddled him. Wanting to be very clear about what he could do, she grabbed one of his hands—still warm from the drink—and placed it on her ass. Then she dropped her lips to his.

He responded immediately. Softly at first, as though feeling her out, as though still struggling to believe this was happening. But after a few strokes, he became almost savage, his lips greedy and demanding. It was such a contrast to his usual demeanor, and she loved it.

When he pulled back, she whimpered. She actually *whimpered*. It was a most distressing sound, but even more distressing was the fact that he was no longer kissing her. She was desperate to feel that connection again.

He chuckled as he took off his glasses and set them next to his mug. There was something filthy and knowing about that chuckle.

She liked how he looked with his glasses, but she also liked how he looked without them. Though perhaps it was what their removal signified more than anything else.

He intended to kiss the shit out of her.

She dropped her mouth once more. She kissed him urgently, and he met her stroke for stroke. He kept his hand firmly on his ass.

Then she pressed her hips against him, and he twisted his head away and groaned.

She experienced an unfamiliar sense of triumph. Ridiculous, but there it was. To think that this man could have such a reaction to her!

She slipped one hand under his flannel shirt and T-shirt and rubbed the warmth of his back. Her other hand drifted to his belly. She wanted to touch every inch of him, and she loved that there was lots to touch.

His mouth moved downward to her neck. She tipped her head back as his beard abraded her sensitive skin, and she ground herself against his erection. Her hands gripped his meaty arms.

*Yes.* This was good. This was real. This was...

"You're so fucking hot," he said.

She froze, his words pulling her out of her lust-filled haze.

It wasn't because she didn't think she was hot.

It wasn't because this was the first time she'd heard Everett swear.

And it wasn't because she couldn't accept compliments. When someone complimented Nora on her work, for example? She believed them. If Aimee or Brianna told her something nice? She didn't doubt their words.

But the last time a man had easily handed out compliments, he'd been using her. He'd conned her out of a few thousand dollars, saying he needed help caring for his sick mother. He'd promised to pay her back soon. Having recently lost her own mother, she'd been in a vulnerable place, and she hadn't thought to question it. Sure, many things were covered by provincial healthcare, but there could easily be other expenses.

After he had the money, she'd never heard from him again, even though she'd talked to him every day for weeks. They'd met in person a few times, too, and everything had been great—or so she'd thought.

Later, she wondered if he'd hoped to get more out of her, if he'd thought she was richer than she actually was.

"Nora?" Everett's voice sounded far away. His hands were no longer touching her; he was gripping the arms of the recliner. "Are you okay?"

"I..." She scrambled up from his lap. "Yeah. I'm fine. I just...you know...I'm not sure about this." She gestured between them. "Not because you did anything wrong, but I..."

He scrubbed a hand over his face and put his glasses back on. That broke her. He didn't deserve this, except what did she know? Maybe he did. She'd heard of men who were lovely partners, only to show their true colors months—or years—later. In some respects, she'd been lucky; what happened with Samuel could have been much worse.

She drained the rest of her drink. It was more like lukewarm buttered rum now, but she wasn't going to let it go to waste.

"I'm sorry," she said, thinking back to several minutes ago, when he'd uttered the same words. "I'm sorry."

Then she grabbed Dino and ran out the door.

# Chapter 9

*Who hurt you, Nora?*

Wednesday morning, as Everett got ready for work, he wondered that for approximately the two-hundredth and fifty-seventh time. It was a good thing he didn't have a sculpture planned until tomorrow. He wouldn't have been able to concentrate well enough to pull it off.

He kept thinking about how she'd sipped her drink, about how she'd launched herself at him and ground herself against him until he'd almost come in his pants.

Then he'd spoken for the first time in minutes, and somehow, that had ruined it for her.

*You're so fucking hot.*

He'd replayed those words over and over in his mind.

Had they been too crude for her? He doubted it. No, it seemed like she struggled with a compliment about her appearance—or a compliment from him, in particular? He wanted to understand, but he wouldn't push her to explain. She'd made it sound like the problem was her, not him, and he hated to think what was going through her head as she fled his apartment. She usually seemed in control of herself, but Sunday had been different.

That evening, he'd sent her a single text. He'd typed and deleted it seven times, and what he'd sent still wasn't quite right, but he'd been unable to find the correct words.

> **Everett:** I'm sorry for how things ended. Don't worry, I'll keep my distance, but if you want to talk, you know where to find me.

He hadn't seen her since, but that was nothing unusual: before he'd run into her at the first snow sculpture, he'd only seen her every few weeks.

He knew he had to give her space. If they encountered each other in the hall, that was one thing, but he wouldn't seek her out, even if she was constantly on his mind. He'd wait for her to come to him.

Everett poured his coffee into a Santa mug and sat down with a bowl of cereal. In an attempt to forget about Nora, he picked up his phone and came across a photo of the walrus sculpture, surrounded by orange fencing.

As if that would stop anyone who wanted to destroy a snow sculpture.

He cleaned his dirty dishes before putting on his clothes for work. Christmas was almost here, and it was his favorite time of year. Even though he'd be spending the twenty-fifth alone, it was a wonderful season. His plan was, overall, a success. His sculptures had turned out just as he'd imagined, and people were enjoying them.

He'd do his best to focus on the good things in life.

Nora was not in a good mood.

Earlier, she'd signed out an ebook from the library, and after a few minutes of reading, she'd started to get a strange feeling about the book. Something wasn't quite right, and a little internet sleuthing revealed that yes, the text was likely AI-generated.

For fuck's sake. Was it so wrong that she wished to relax with a novel written by an actual human?

She wanted to read stories that had been written with care, by a writer who'd wrestled with words, who might have sworn at the computer and procrastinated by cleaning the entire apartment and furiously dictated notes in the middle of the night; she didn't want to simply consume content for the sake of it. So, she'd pulled an old favorite off her shelf, unwilling to take a chance on anything new. If she found an AI prompt in a book, she'd probably chuck something at the wall.

And now, she was in a Christmas-themed pop-up bar, seated next to a very large nutcracker. There was a young couple to her left, and a group of women in their thirties to her right. It wasn't making her feel any less cranky.

"I'm not sure why you wanted to come here," she muttered.

"I know it's not your thing, but the drinks are good, aren't they?" Aimee took a sip of hers. It was a violent shade of red.

Or a seasonally appropriate shade of red, as others might say. But Nora was feeling rather violent at the moment. Everything was making her angry today. When she'd been spending time with Everett, she hadn't been quite as irritated with life in general, but then he'd uttered those words...

She tried her own drink. It was a twist on an old-fashioned—as in, the least offensively Christmasy thing on the menu—and it was decent. But, to her frustration, it wasn't as good as the drink that her neighbor had made her.

"Yeah," she said. "Sure."

When Aimee frowned, Nora felt annoyed with herself for bringing down her friend's good spirits. Aimee's night with her new man had been amazing. She had that glowing *I'm-in-love, I-just-had-sex* look.

Nora shouldn't find it quite so nauseating, but she did. "Tell me more about—"

"No," Aimee said. "I want to know why you're even grumpier than usual."

"Am not," Nora protested instinctively.

Aimee gave her a withering look.

Nora sighed. She considered bringing up the library book, but in all honesty, that wasn't the main reason for her bad mood. "The guy across the hall from me. His name is Everett. I ran into him when I went to see the first snow sculpture—you know, the one that I assumed was AI? Anyway, we've been spending time together ever since."

"'Spending time together.'" Aimee used air quotes.

"We went to see the other snow sculptures."

"That sounds very cute," Aimee said. "Wholesome. I can't believe you actually saw them all."

"Yes. Well."

"I'm glad you're enjoying the season, rather than punishing yourself with a second job."

"I wasn't punishing myself," Nora said. "I was making back the money I'd lost."

"But I suspect that wasn't the only reason, and I was afraid you'd get a retail job again this December, even though you've earned back all the money. Instead, you're seeing Everett." Aimee's voice was gentle. "What happened with him?"

Nora didn't mention the time he'd collapsed in the hallway. "We made out on Sunday. It was...well, it was good. Then he *complimented* me."

"Was there something wrong with the compliment?"

"No. I just..." Nora looked down at the giant ice cube in her drink. "I freaked out and left. Because suddenly...I couldn't help wondering what he wanted from me. How he might try to manipulate me."

"Nora..." Aimee reached over and patted her shoulder.

"He hasn't done anything to warrant that response. He's been sweet and not at all pushy, but I haven't known him that long. Like, I've lived across from him for two years, but we barely spoke until this month, and I'm a terrible judge of character."

"One mistake doesn't make you a terrible judge of character."

"But that was one very big mistake!" She couldn't forgive herself for falling for a scam. Her, of all people. Even in the midst of her grief, she should have known better. "Anyway, Everett's not like him, but I can't help worrying. I..."

She trailed off as "We Wish You a Merry Christmas" started playing. She hated this song.

"Right," she said. "What was I saying? Oh yes, it was the first time I'd made out with someone since Samuel, and Samuel—if that was even his real name—was always very complimentary. Overly so, in retrospect. I thought he'd just fallen hard, but of course, that wasn't the case. It was silly to believe someone could genuinely say those things about me."

"Well, first of all, that's not true. You're hot. Plus, you're kind and supportive and adorably bad-tempered."

Nora snorted.

"So, Everett paid you a single compliment while you were making out..."

"And I couldn't trust it. Yeah." Nora shook her head. "I don't know what I was thinking. I swore I wouldn't get involved with anyone again, and here I am."

"Did you really think you'd swear it off forever?"

"Yes," Nora said. "I did. But he was like...thawing my soul, or some such nonsense. I wanted things that I hadn't wanted in a long time."

Which was what had gotten her into trouble two and a half years ago, that craving for a connection. Loneliness could be a dangerous feeling; she should have known better than to act on it.

"Physical things?" Aimee asked. "Or other things?"

Nora froze—but in a different way from the other night.

Her friend had made a good point. Nora had been thinking of sex and romance as intertwined because that was how it had always worked for her in the past.

But why did it have to be that way? Maybe she and Everett could just have something physical. She could have a little fun and get it out of her system. It wasn't completely risk-free, but she'd make sure that Aimee knew where she was. There was nothing wrong with having a few orgasms that weren't thanks to her vibrator or her fingers. She could keep those high barriers around her heart firmly in place.

If Everett complimented her again—though he might be afraid to do so—she'd assume his motive was to get in her pants. Something she wanted as well.

"You're right." Nora downed the rest of her drink. "Some no-strings-attached sex will do me good."

"Is that what you *want*?" Aimee asked. "Or—"

"Yes," Nora said. "It is."

# Chapter 10

WHEN EVERETT RETURNED HOME on Thursday night—or, rather, the wee hours of Friday morning—he was in much better shape than he'd been after the previous snow sculpture. The unicorn with the sprig of holly on her horn had taken him just as long as the last one, but he'd eaten more beforehand, this time ordering a dinner for two from a nearby Indian restaurant. As he'd remembered, it was more like a dinner for three. After finishing his last bite of biryani and a bottle of water, he'd polished off a Deep'n Delicious cake, then headed out with a bag of snacks and drinks in case he needed them.

He'd eaten a granola bar while he worked, and he was in no danger of passing out as he reached for the keys in his pocket. He was about to enter his apartment when he thought he heard a noise from Nora's unit, but maybe he'd imagined it.

He slept soundly and woke up at eleven thirty—he'd used a vacation day, so he hadn't set an alarm. Once again, he found himself thinking of Nora. Had she seen pictures of the sculpture? Did she like it? Would she ask to see this one with him? It seemed doubtful, but a man could hope.

As he ate an omelet, he read what people were saying online. One man said he'd walked his dog through the park at ten thirty at night, and there was no sculpture then. But at six thirty the next morning, there it was.

A homeless man who slept in the park had talked to a reporter. He said the sculpture had just appeared. One moment, there was nothing, and the next...a unicorn. Like magic.

Everett didn't recall seeing the man, and nobody seemed to believe his story, but it was quite accurate.

A discussion about the sculpture devolved into a heated argument about unicorns, but most comments were positive. A few people likened whoever was responsible for the sculptures to Santa Claus, and he appreciated the comparison. Naturally, there was speculation about whether there would be any more sculptures before Christmas next week.

Spoiler: there would be one more.

There was also speculation about whether the people behind the sculptures would eventually reveal themselves.

Spoiler: they would not.

Nobody would believe the truth, and Everett was happy to remain anonymous. Actually, he preferred it; he'd never loved having lots of attention.

But there was one exception. The sculptures seemed to penetrate Nora's adorably Grinchy spirit and make her smile, and he wanted her to know it was him. Plus, there was something lonely about being the only person who had the full story. He wished someone else could be in on the secret.

He knew, however, that she'd refuse to believe it, and so he'd keep his mouth shut.

That evening, Everett piped royal icing onto the gingerbread cookies he'd made earlier. As he worked, he couldn't help wondering what Nora was doing. Was she lounging around her apartment in the hippo pajama pants that he vaguely remembered from the other night? He wanted to ask if she was okay, but he'd promised he wouldn't bother her, and he'd keep his promise.

Except he kept thinking of how she'd felt in his lap. The eager way she'd kissed him, her breathy sighs...

There was a knock at his door, and his hand slipped.

"Shit," he muttered. The little gingerbread man now had a weird slash across his leg.

Still, he couldn't be too upset because it was most likely Nora.

He walked to the door and opened it up.

And there she was, wearing a sweater and jeans, her hair loose. The set of her chin was firm, as though she'd come to a decision. As though she meant business.

But the first words out of her mouth were an apology.

"Once again," she said, "I'm sorry. I know it was ridiculous to freak out because you paid me a compliment. I don't want to get into it, but due to something that happened with…an ex, I can't trust men who try to charm me in any way."

Everett had never considered using his powers for violence before, but he wanted to bury that asshole in an avalanche. He also wanted to promise he wasn't like her ex.

Before he could decide whether to say those words out loud—he worried they would sound meaningless, especially when he didn't even know what had happened—she continued.

"But I've decided…I want this. I want to start where we left off. If you're interested."

"Yes," he said without hesitation. "Absolutely. Shall I make some hot buttered rum?"

"I don't think that'll be necessary."

She launched herself at him, and he couldn't help smiling. When he picked her up, his hands under her ass, she wrapped her arms around his neck and kissed him hard; he loved her enthusiasm. He walked backward as he returned the kiss, bumping into the coffee table before finding his way to the recliner where they'd made out last time. Once they were seated, he slid one hand to her breast. When she groaned, his hand dove under her sweater, and he fingered the bead of her nipple through her bra.

In one almost-smooth move, she pulled her sweater, tank top, and bra over her head and dropped them on the floor...and all he could do was stare.

*You're so beautiful.*

But he didn't say that, even though staying silent made him ache.

Instead, he'd show her.

He took off his glasses so they wouldn't get in the way, and then he pulled her nipple into his mouth. She gave a little squeak of pleasure and tipped her head back.

He wanted to do everything to her all at once, but unfortunately, he only had so many hands—and only one mouth. He moved to her other breast, biting lightly before soothing her with his tongue. His hands roamed up her back before shifting to her sides, her stomach, the underswell of her breasts. His movements were halted by her removal of his flannel shirt, quickly followed by the removal of his T-shirt. But then he captured her mouth again, smiling when she sighed in bliss against his lips.

"Everett..."

She didn't say anything else, but just his name, in her voice, shot another bolt of desire through him.

Then she did something much, much worse.

She began grinding against him, like she had on Sunday. Rubbing against his cock at an angle that was, frankly, dangerous. He wasn't sure how long he could last.

"Oh my..." he stuttered.

At his lack of coherence, a wicked grin tugged at her lips. As much as he loved it, he was also desperate to wipe it off her face. He unbuttoned her jeans and hurriedly slid his hand inside her underwear, needing to feel how wet she was for him.

He wasn't disappointed.

He bit his lip—so hard he nearly drew blood—to stop himself from telling her, once again, how fucking hot she looked. And then he smiled because he'd certainly succeeded in wiping away that grin.

"Everett," she panted.

He slid two fingers inside her, and the groan that escaped her mouth was completely obscene.

She rode his hand and palmed her breasts. It was such a fucking gift. Her pupils were blown, her lips parted, and he could look at this all day. She was normally a little guarded, reluctant to share herself, but not now.

Now she was open to him.

Then she dropped her hand and grasped his erection through his jeans. In response, he shoved his fingers even deeper inside her, and she lost her rhythm. She tried to get it back, but she faltered when he rubbed her clit.

"Ev…" She didn't finish saying his name. No, she dropped her head and bit his shoulder as she shuddered around his fingers.

Everett was overcome with pride. Pride that he could make her feel this way. He eased his fingers out of her, and he was about to ask if she'd like to take this to the bedroom when she did something unexpected.

She stripped off the rest of her clothes and started grinding against him again.

"You're going to make me…" he began.

"I know," she said, but she paused her movements.

*Fuck.*

When he nodded, she gripped his shoulders and kissed him as she moved, faster and faster. He'd lost all control of this situation, and somehow, he didn't mind. Her bare breasts were mashed against his chest as her tongue wrestled with his, and he climbed toward that inevitable release.

"Nora…"

# Chapter 11

Once they'd cleaned themselves up, they retreated to Everett's bed. Unlike his living room, his bedroom was free of festive cheer, aside from a small Santa figurine beside his alarm clock. Nora smiled at it before looking at Everett.

"I'm not twenty-one anymore," he said. "I'm not sure I'll be ready to do it again tonight."

"That's okay. You can focus on making me feeling good," she said saucily.

But if he just wanted to cozy up together, that was fine, too. There was always tomorrow.

"By the way, how old *are* you?" she asked.

"Thirty-five."

That was about what she'd assumed. A five-year difference at her age? It was nothing. Perfectly appropriate for a relationship, not that she wanted one of those. This was just a little friendly sex. She'd get it out of her system soon enough.

The last time she'd had sex with a guy, she'd felt gross after it was all over, after she'd realized he was only using her for money. But that wouldn't happen here. She had no expectations; she knew exactly what she was getting into.

"One sec." She pulled her phone out of her discarded jeans and sent a quick text to Aimee, just letting her friend know where she planned to spend the night. Then she curled up on her side, facing Everett. "Now I'm all yours."

He shot her a lopsided grin and ran a hand up her body, his thumb stroking over her breast. Without the urgency of before, but that he was okay. Clearly, he was still very much enjoying himself. In return, she ran her fingers through the hair on his chest. There was something beautiful about exploring someone else's nakedness for the first time.

"I do want to make you feel good," he murmured.

Those quiet words were enough to send a shiver of anticipation down her spine.

Lazily, he slid his hand lower. Like he was moving through molasses. Like he had all the time in the world.

She did not. She'd gone so long without another person touching her like this, and she hadn't realized how much she craved it.

"Please," she said.

The corner of his mouth quirked up again. He ran his thick finger over her entrance, and when she moaned in desperation and squirmed against him, he took pity on her and slid it inside.

"*Ohhh.*"

This, too, made his lips quirk up. A private smile, just for her.

He kept his finger inside her as he dove under the blankets. A moment later, his tongue...oh my god. How was he doing that? She didn't understand how it felt so amazing. It should be impossible for anything to feel this good.

"*Please*," she said, with more desperation than before.

He looked up at her, which was exactly what she didn't want, even if she did like seeing his lips coated in her moisture.

Nora shoved his head back down, and she felt his soft laughter against her sensitive flesh before he began pleasuring her again, twisting his finger as he worked her with his tongue. She'd forgotten just how amazing this could feel...or maybe it had never felt quite this amazing before.

She bucked against his face. He sucked on her clit, and...and...

She shattered.

When she came back to herself, he was no longer between her legs but lying next to her. She climbed on top of him and kissed him. The kiss quickly turned from gentle to searing, and his cock stirred beneath her.

"Hm." She slid down his body and took his growing erection between her lips, gratified when he hardened further almost immediately. She glanced up at his face, the tip still in her mouth; he had his hand on his forehead.

She increased her efforts, enjoying his response, until he grasped her upper arm and hauled her up.

"Do you want me to come in your mouth?" He sounded almost stern—and she wasn't used to that side of him.

"Not today."

*How many times do you think this is going to happen, Nora?*

She pushed that thought aside. "Do you have condoms?"

He nodded, reached into his bedside table, and pulled out...not condoms.

"Shit," he said, getting out of bed. He threw a bunch of things onto the floor in his haste to find what he was looking for. Painkillers, several sheets of paper, three books of puzzles, two familiar Christmas ornaments... "There."

She almost whimpered in relief.

"I still need to find the lube," he said.

"No, you don't. I'm wet enough." And she certainly didn't want to wait any longer.

Fortunately, he wasted no time in rolling on the condom and positioning himself above her. He slid inside in one smooth motion, and it was glorious. His thick cock filled her just right, and she wrapped her arms and legs around him and urged him to move. He braced himself on his elbows as he began thrusting.

"You're not going to crush me, don't worry." She wanted to feel more of him, to be consumed by him.

He allowed her to take more of his weight as he thrust again, deeper than before.

"Yes," she murmured. "*Yes.*"

She had a strange premonition that he was going to compliment her. She wasn't sure she could take it, even if he just said she felt good, so she raised her mouth to his and kissed him. Drowned in his lips as she met him thrust for thrust. Lost herself in the physical sensation of being joined with another person, something she hadn't allowed herself in a long, long time. His touch felt like such a fundamental part of her.

An infuriating voice in her brain whispered that once or twice wouldn't be enough, but she pushed that aside by pressing herself harder against him, by stroking her tongue against his. She'd just be in the moment and take everything she could.

He reached between them to finger her clit...and her third orgasm of the evening caught her off guard, somehow even stronger than the other two.

She held him close as he found his release inside her.

When Everett returned from the washroom, he was relieved to see Nora under his sheets. He'd been half afraid that she'd already be pulling on her clothes, ready to escape across the hall.

But no, she was here.

"Do you want to stay the night?" he asked.

He desperately wanted her to, but if she didn't, he wouldn't push.

When she nodded, he couldn't contain his grin.

Nobody had slept over at his place in well over a year, and that seemed like a distant memory now. All he could think about was Nora.

After she took her turn in the washroom, she put on her underwear. "Do you have a shirt I could sleep in?"

"Middle drawer, on the right," he said.

She grabbed one of his white undershirts and pulled it over her head. The shirt hung just above her knees, and it was erotic to see her in his clothes. She was fucking sexy and it felt so fucking good to be inside her—not that he'd say such things.

He hoped they'd get there eventually, though. He wanted to keep her in his life, and not just as a neighbor he occasionally greeted in the hallway.

She wrapped an arm around him and rested her head on his shoulder, and he was hopeful she felt the same way.

When Nora woke up the next morning, she was disoriented. It had been ages since she'd slept anywhere but her own bed. Everett was on his side, facing away from her, and she had the urge to cuddle up against him, but she feared it would wake him, and she didn't want to do that. It was only seven on a Saturday.

However, she did have to use the washroom, so she climbed out of bed as quietly as she could. Everett didn't stir.

When she returned to the bedroom, she noticed all the things that were strewn across the floor, including the ornaments he'd received a couple of weeks ago. She wondered if he'd eventually gotten the right ones—she hadn't asked. Naked Santa, with a striped stocking over his dick, leered at her. She felt compelled to tidy everything up, but...

Wait a second.

She picked up a sheet of paper. The sketch looked curiously like one of the snow sculptures, the one with the hockey-playing bears.

Nora's first thought was that he'd drawn it from a photograph, but why were there multiple measurements and notes on the page?

Her stomach dropped.

He had to be responsible for the sculptures.

# Chapter 12

As Nora stared at the sketch in her hand, her annoyance grew. She looked at the floor and noticed another drawing, this one of the walrus. Again, there were lots of measurements and notes, and it looked like the paper had been folded up. Everett must have taken it with him to the park.

He'd lied to her. Just like Samuel.

She shook her head. This wasn't the same. But she still felt like Everett should have told her. They'd seen many of the sculptures together—why had he gone in the first place? To observe people's reactions? And hadn't she asked who he thought was behind it?

It wasn't the same as lying to steal from her, but she was pissed nonetheless. It felt like a big lie by omission when their entire "relationship" had centered around those sculptures.

*It's okay,* she told herself. *You were prepared for the worst. That's why you never intended to have anything lasting with him.*

Except, if she was honest with herself, some part of her had wanted more. She'd tried to deny it, but it was true.

God, she couldn't handle this. She'd get dressed, hurry back to her apartment, and call Aimee. She couldn't—

"Nora?"

*Shit.*

She whirled around. Everett was sitting up in bed.

"What are you doing?" he asked as he put on his glasses.

"You lied to me," she said before she could think better of it. She held up the drawings.

He shut his eyes and looked pained. He didn't refute it.

Ha! She felt a spark of triumph that quickly deflated.

"You're one of the people behind the snow sculptures," she continued, trying to ignore the empty ache inside her.

"It's not what you think," he said.

She gave him an incredulous look. "Oh really. These are just drawings you did after you saw them? Then why the measurements?"

"I'm not one of the people responsible. I'm *the* person. The only person."

"Yeah, right. It's impossible for a single person to make one of those sculptures overnight."

"It's possible," he assured her.

"How?"

"Magic."

She snorted...and then she realized he was serious. At least, he was seriously trying to convince her that it was magic. There was no teasing smile on his face.

"You've got to be fucking kidding me." She dropped the drawings and strode to the bedroom door.

"Nora. Wait."

Against her better judgment, she hesitated.

Everett sighed in relief when Nora gingerly sat on the edge of his bed. He wanted to pull her into his arms and hold her while he explained, but he knew she wouldn't like that, so he didn't.

God, if only he'd been more careful while looking for the condoms last night. But he'd been desperate to get inside her, and he hadn't been thinking.

She crossed her arms over her chest. "This ought to be good."

She seemed so far away. He'd thought they were getting closer, and now, it felt like that had all meant nothing.

"I can move snow without touching it," he said.

She snorted again. "Then show me."

"I can't. Nobody else can watch while I do it, like there's a protective shield around me."

"How convenient."

This was such a mess, but he pressed on. "It takes a lot out of me. I have to eat a ton beforehand. The night I collapsed in the hallway? I'd pushed myself too far. Hadn't eaten enough, even though I'd consumed the better part of two pizzas."

There was a flicker of something in her eyes, but then her face hardened.

If only he could turn back the clock and stuff those drawings in the drawer before she found them. Then maybe he could be holding her right now and pressing kisses to her neck.

Alas, that wasn't the kind of magic he could do. He could only work with snow, not time.

"What's next?" she asked. "You gonna claim you're Santa Claus?"

"I'm not Santa Claus."

"There we go. Finally, something true."

This wasn't Nora, not the Nora he knew. His Nora might be a little tough on the outside, but she was delighted by...

Wait. Why was he thinking of her as *his*?

"I was a fool before," she said. "I believed a man's lies, but I won't do that again."

"It's the truth, I swear. I didn't tell you earlier because I'd never told anyone. I knew no one would believe me." And clearly, he'd been right.

But why did this have to happen with *Nora*?

She sighed. "Look. I don't know what's happening with you, but I can't do this. I can't get involved. I was only planning on spending a night or two with you anyway. Turn around while I get changed, and don't stop me from leaving."

He turned away from her, his shoulders slumped, and forced himself to keep breathing. It was a blow to know that even before the last five minutes, she'd never thought this could last. He'd wanted to walk around the city together in the winter and then the spring, her hand in his, and find new ways to make her smile.

Had she never thought of such things? Or perhaps she had, but it had distressed her because of whatever had happened in her past.

"You can look now," she said.

She stood at the door to his bedroom. She was going to walk out and never talk to him again, aside from a perfunctory greeting, and he couldn't stand it. He had to do something. Convince her that he wasn't a liar, at the very least. He refused to be lumped in the same category as her ex, and he wanted—needed—her to believe that there was honesty in the world.

"What if I try to show you?" he asked.

# Chapter 13

"You just told me that was impossible." Nora crossed her arms over her chest.

This guy really was a piece of work. And to think she'd started to trust him! She couldn't believe she'd been so naïve.

"You can't see me move the snow," Everett said. "But maybe if you see how quickly I can make a snow sculpture appear, you'll have to believe."

Well, she didn't *have* to do anything, but a part of her was tempted; a part of her wanted to believe he wasn't lying to her. Because if this unlikely story *was* true, then it was understandable that he wouldn't tell anyone unless absolutely necessary. If she had such powers, she'd keep them a secret, too.

"Fine," she said, "but you have to let me bring a friend. I won't go anywhere alone with you."

"As long as your friend promises not to talk to anyone about what they see."

He'd agreed to her terms, and so she'd do this.

"When?" she asked. "I'd rather not do it at night."

He named a park near where they lived. "Three o'clock. You and your friend can meet me there. By the trees, away from the playground."

As Nora approached the meeting spot with Aimee, she could see Everett's large form, clad in his red winter coat, and her heart sped up.

Mentally, she told herself to calm the fuck down.

"I still can't believe," Aimee said, "that he claimed he could do *magic*."

"Yeah," Nora agreed. "It's ridiculous."

It was a gray winter's day, and the snow wasn't as pretty as it had once been. The roads were lined with dirty snowbanks. It didn't look like something that would appear on a Christmas card.

But here, in the park, it was a little better. It was cold and windy, though, and there were few people out. Nobody else was near the location that Everett had chosen.

"Aimee, this is Everett," Nora said when they stopped in front of him. "Everett, Aimee."

They shook hands and Everett smiled, but it wavered slightly.

*He's nervous.*

Nora steeled herself. She would not be affected by him.

"What do you want me to make?" he asked.

"Just a snowman," she said.

He nodded. Then he took a few steps away from her, held up his hands...and vanished.

Nora and Aimee looked at each other.

"You can't see him, can you?" Nora asked.

Aimee's mouth hung open. "I can't."

As soon as she spoke, Everett reappeared, along with a snowman. There was less snow on the ground in his vicinity—he must have used the existing snow for his magic. Nora walked toward the snowman and touched it, needing to convince herself that it wasn't an illusion.

"What did you see?" Everett asked.

"You disappeared, then reappeared with a snowman thirty seconds later." She didn't look at him, just continued to stare at the snowman.

But what if he still wasn't telling the truth? What if time moved differently when he disappeared, and what felt like thirty seconds to her had been fifteen minutes to him?

Either way, he could still perform magic.

"Now do something more complicated," Aimee said. "Prove you really could be the one behind the sculptures. Make us a giant seal."

Everett shook his head. "I have to prepare for something big. But you know the rabbits by the fire in the third sculpture? I can make a smaller one of those."

"Okay, that'll do."

Once again, Nora stood next to her friend and watched as Everett disappeared. She couldn't sort through everything going on in her head. It was a mess.

It would have been simpler if his claims of magic had been false. She'd know what to do with that discovery: she'd walk away and never speak to him again unless absolutely necessary. She'd lump him in with Samuel and the people who made answering phone calls a pointless endeavor. She'd make the walls around her heart even higher. But now...

She felt a hand on her shoulder.

"Are you okay?" Aimee asked.

"I...I don't know."

"That's partly why I asked him to make something else. To buy us—you—a little time."

Nora shut her eyes and relaxed against her friend. Yes, there were so many scams in the world, so many people spouting absolute nonsense. For their own gain...or in some cases, online scammers were victims of human trafficking.

It was frustrating to always be wondering if what you saw or heard was fake, and technology had given rise to new ways of deceiving others.

But there were real things in her life, too. Like this friendship with Aimee.

"What are you going to do now?" Aimee asked gently.

"I don't know," Nora said again.

"Before you found the sketch, did you feel like you'd gotten him out of your system?"

"No." Nora sighed. "I want more, but even knowing that he wasn't lying about this..." She gestured toward the snowman. "It doesn't mean he won't try to screw me over."

It was hard to imagine Everett Sun ever screwing anyone over, but she still had to be vigilant.

"I know," Aimee said, "but maybe it's worth—holy shit."

Nora jerked her head around and saw Everett standing next to a small rabbit—a bit higher than his waist—made of snow. Like the other sculptures they'd seen together, it made her smile.

There could be no doubt now: he really was behind all the delightful snow sculptures.

Yes, sometimes the unbelievable was real. A tightly wound part of her began to loosen.

"I'm always here if you need anything," Aimee said, "but would you like me to go now?"

"Yeah," Nora said, her gaze still locked on the sculpture. "You can go."

Aimee waved at Everett.

"Nice to meet you," he called out before coming to stand next to Nora.

His proximity made her skin prickle, and she swallowed before meeting his eyes.

"All the sculptures across the city," she said. "Why did you do it?"

"I'd wanted to for years, and this year, there was finally enough snow in Toronto before Christmas for it to work."

"You could have moved somewhere else. Montreal. Quebec City. St. John's."

"But then I wouldn't have met you." His serious, quiet tone made goose bumps break out on her skin.

"You still didn't answer my question," she said. "Why did you do it?"

"To make people feel a bit of Christmas magic."

"It certainly worked on me." She hoped that didn't sound sarcastic; she was sincere.

He scrubbed a hand over his face. "That's why I ran into you at the first sculpture—I wanted to see people experiencing it. I'm sorry I didn't tell you earlier, but I—"

"No, that's okay. I understand why you didn't say anything. It's just...I was the victim of a romance scam." She looked down. "More than two years ago—it was shortly after my mother died. I hadn't been with anyone since then. That's why I freaked out when you complimented me. I kept hearing his voice. Recalling how gross I felt afterward, when I remembered that we'd been intimate."

Everett's gloved hand was underneath her chin now, but he didn't tip it up, didn't force her to meet his eyes. "I'm so sorry."

"I have some trust issues. Obviously, you telling me that you could do magic is a very different situation, but I still couldn't help thinking..."

Well, now she was thinking that she should see a therapist.

"Can I hold you?" he asked.

She nodded, already snuggling against the bulk of him. His touch grounded her.

"I'd never try to scam you," he said, "but I know you may struggle to believe that right now. I know it'll take time for you to fully trust me."

"It might take a lot of time, but I think I want to try."

Although it was terrifying to say those words, she meant them. Her life had contracted in the past few years. She'd kept it small to avoid risk, but it hadn't healed the gaping emptiness inside of her, and she didn't want to live like that forever. The time she'd spent with Everett had been a revelation.

Nora swiped at the tears collecting in her eyelashes, then tilted her head up to his. His lips met hers in a gentle kiss that she could feel down to her toes. It warmed every part of her.

She pulled back and let out a shuddering breath. "I think I'd like to head home," she said, clutching his arm.

"Could you wait a few minutes? I want to make one more thing for you."

He lifted his other arm, and after a moment of holding it out, snow lifted from the ground, as if by magic.

No, it *was* magic. She could see it happening, unlike before, and the snow sparkled in the air. It was incredible.

*Holy shit.*

He raised the arm she was holding, but she didn't let go, though she loosened her grip. She suspected that the physical contact was the reason she could see this, but she didn't say anything; she wasn't even certain she'd be capable of speaking, and besides, she didn't want to disrupt his work. Though she wasn't sure what he was making, she didn't care. No matter the final product, this was mesmerizing.

A magically generated snow sculpture.

Nora stared as it took shape. Everett removed some snow from the bottom to create a heart. It was about twenty centimeters thick, standing on its end.

"Wow," she said.

His head snapped toward her. "You can see it?"

# Chapter 14

"You're making a heart," Nora said.

He frowned. Nobody had ever been able to see him do this before. Even earlier, she hadn't seen the process; she'd just seen the result. Why…

*Oh.* She was touching him. That had to be it.

All this time, he'd thought it was impossible to show someone else what he could do, but apparently, there had been a way all along.

Or was it only with her?

Either way, he was glad that she could watch. He smoothed the perimeter of the heart, making sure it was perfectly symmetrical, then lowered his arms. As usual, there was a *whoosh*.

Nora fumbled in her bag, and a moment later, she held up a granola bar. "Eat. I don't want you passing out again."

He couldn't protest when she used that bossy tone. He took off his glove, opened the wrapper, and ate the granola bar in a few bites.

Everett wasn't sure whether she always had one of those in her purse, or whether she'd brought it just for him, despite her doubts about his story. But he did know that she took care of the people who were close to her, even if she frequently emitted standoffish vibes.

And now he knew why.

It hurt to think of how that man had used her. She hadn't provided details, but it was enough to understand why she struggled to trust people and believe compliments.

He hoped that, one day soon, she'd moan in his bed as he praised every single part of her. He'd seen it all last night—and it was certainly worthy of praise.

"I'm sorry I was angry that you kept the truth from me," she said, "but I understand why you did. It was such an outrageous story—"

"Which is why I understood your doubts."

"The kind of story that's so wild, it almost *has* to be true. Because why would someone make that up?"

"I don't know," he said, "but people lie about all sorts of things."

"Yet you're not as cynical as I am."

"I like your cynical, Christmas-hating ass." He grinned.

"I wouldn't go so far as to say I *hate* Christmas, but some things about it do get to me."

"Ah, you're already coming around. Next thing you know, you'll be taking sleigh rides and belting out 'We Wish You a Merry Christmas.'"

She responded with an exaggerated shudder.

Yes, she was delightful.

"Let's go home," he said, "but I'd like to destroy the snow sculptures before we do. You can take pictures of them first, but they're not part of my grand plan, and I feel weird about leaving them up. Aside from the snowman, that is."

Nora took a picture before kicking the middle of the heart. She knocked off the rabbit's head, then jabbed it in the stomach.

"Now, after all that violence," she said, "I could use some hot buttered rum."

A few days later, after eating fried chicken and two boxes of Kraft Dinner, Everett headed out to make his last snow sculpture, as planned.

But this time, he wasn't alone.

He'd shown Nora his design—two owls snuggling in a wreath—and asked if she had any suggestions. She'd said she liked it just as it was.

Now, she stood behind him, her arms wrapped around his middle, as he moved the snow. In her bag, she had some Christmas cookies, as well as a thermos of hot chocolate. It wasn't as chilly as some of the other nights that Everett had been out, but the cold still got to him when he was outside for hours.

Her touch, however, did help.

At two in the morning, they returned to the apartment building. He was still a little weak, but he was buoyed by the fact that he'd completed his plan...and that Nora was next to him. He was so glad he could share this with her, and he hoped to share more with her, too.

After taking a deep breath, he asked the question that had been on his mind for a while.

"Would you like to spend Christmas with me?"

A few weeks ago, Nora had thought she'd be spending Christmas alone for the first time. Her mother was gone. Brianna's family was visiting her husband's relatives. Aimee was visiting her father. And while Christmas wasn't Nora's favorite time of year, the thought had still filled her with dread. She'd viewed the holiday season as something she'd have to survive, not something she could enjoy.

But as it turned out, she didn't have to be alone after all.

The lights on the Christmas tree twinkled in Everett's apartment, and a small ham and some potatoes were baking in the oven. Christmas music was playing, but Everett had thoughtfully removed her least-favorite songs from the playlist. Dino—and his red bow—kept watch over the room from the recliner.

It was very Christmasy in here, but outside was a different matter.

Everett's lovely owl sculpture hadn't lasted long. Not two days later, it had started to melt as the temperature climbed well above freezing, and the rain had started yesterday. A few pictures of the ruined sculptures had surfaced on social media.

It would have been nice to have a white Christmas, rather than watching the rain stream down the windows. It would have been nice for those sculptures to last just a little longer.

But as Nora snuggled against Everett, she couldn't complain. In a world of lies and misinformation, there was still hope. She couldn't be certain that whatever they had would last, but she didn't want to be someone who never tried anything new, who barely even talked to anyone new. She'd be careful and plan for the worst, but she'd also do her best to trust that things could get better.

She bit off the head of a gingerbread man. In her opinion, that was the best way to eat them: starting with the head.

"You're a monster," Everett muttered fondly.

Once she'd finished consuming her gingerbread man, his mouth swooped in before she could decapitate another one. He tasted of spice and evergreen, and his beard scraped against her skin in the most pleasing of ways.

She hadn't expected to fall for someone like him: a man who wanted to bring Christmas cheer to people he didn't even know.

Well, to be honest, she hadn't expected to fall for anyone ever again, but certainly not for someone who'd bake gingerbread while whistling "Carol of the Bells."

But he was simply amazing, and while most of the city engaged in wild speculation about the snow sculptures, she was one of the very few who knew the truth.

Though he might be able to work with snow much faster than a regular person, his sculptures were still done with care and intentionality. They were a way of connecting people, and they'd helped bring Nora and Everett together.

His hand slipped under her shirt, and she moaned softly against him.

"Hold that thought," he murmured. "I think the food is ready."

He started to get up, but she pulled him back down for a kiss.

"Merry Christmas," she whispered against his lips. "Merry, merry Christmas."

# Epilogue

***Five years later***

WHEN NORA BLACKBURN WOKE up on Christmas morning, she turned to the sleeping man next to her. He was lying on his side, his lips parted slightly. There was a little gray in his beard now, which she rather liked.

The alarm would go off in five minutes, and she'd let him sleep until then. Though she wouldn't normally set an alarm for Christmas morning, they had to get the large turkey in the oven at a decent hour. Another year, they'd do a ham, but Nora had wanted to try something different this holiday. She smiled wistfully as she thought of her mother putting a ham in the oven; she wished her mom could have met Everett.

While it was their sixth Christmas together, it would be their first year hosting Christmas for her family. It was also their first Christmas in their new house. They'd bought the small home in the summer, and Nora loved it.

When she and Everett had first started dating, she'd hoped that, one day, they'd be able to build a life together, but she hadn't wanted to rush into anything, and he'd been patient. It would have been convenient—and cost-effective—for them to live together sooner, but they'd waited almost three years to move into a two-bedroom apartment in their old building.

And now, they owned this place with its garland-covered bannisters. They had a large Christmas tree downstairs, as well as red and green lights outside. There was also a small tree on one of the bedside tables.

The past couple of winters had been warm, so there hadn't been many snow sculptures. Three years ago, Everett made a giant sea lion before Christmas, and the city debated whether it was the work of the same person as the previous sculptures, or someone new. He didn't want too many people to know about his powers, but when his parents and brother had visited Toronto, he'd demonstrated his magic for them.

Previously, Nora had wondered if other members of his family had similar abilities that they'd never shared, but apparently not. Still, she suspected he wasn't the only person in the world who could do something that ought to be impossible.

Everett opened his eyes. "Hey. What time is it?"

"The alarm will go off in two minutes."

He pulled her close. "Mm. You feel amazing."

Nora smiled. She no longer tensed when he said such things.

His hands drifted to her thighs. "Do you think two minutes is enough time?"

"For what?"

The next thing she knew—how had he managed it so quickly?—he'd shifted her so she was sitting on his face. He pushed her underwear to the side and set his tongue to her clit.

"You're certainly feeling naughty this morning," she said. "Maybe you're too naughty to get a Christmas present."

His rumble of laughter vibrated pleasantly between her legs. "I thought this would be a nice way to start the day."

That was true, too. Naughty *and* nice. Based on past experience, he'd be able to manage it in under two minutes, especially if he kept...

"*Ahhh*," she cried. "Everett."

He licked her through her climax, just the way she liked it, and as soon as she collapsed on his chest, the alarm went off.

"Ready to start the day?" he asked.

She made some inarticulate noises.

"That's okay," he said. "I'll bring you coffee in bed."

"Have I told you that I love you?"

"You might have brought it up before."

"Well, I'll do it again. I love you." It had taken her a while to say those words, but she never tired of saying them now.

Because what they had together...it was wonderfully real.

In fact, it was so wonderful that it still felt like magic.

# Acknowledgments

Thank you to my editor, Ali Williams, for helping me improve this book and catching my errors, and to Jay Pillerva for the lovely cover. I would also like to thank Cara Luna and Elise Kennedy for beta reading the manuscript.

# About the Author

**Jackie Lau** decided she wanted to be a writer when she was in grade two, sometime between writing "The Heart That Got Lost" and "The Land of Shapes." She later studied engineering and worked as a geophysicist before turning to writing romance novels. Jackie lives in Toronto with her husband, and despite living in Canada her whole life, she hates winter. When she's not writing, she enjoys gelato, gourmet donuts, cooking, hiking, and reading on the balcony when it's raining.

To learn more and sign up for her newsletter, visit jackielaubooks.com.

# Also by Jackie Lau

*Love, Lies, and Cherry Pie*

*Time Loops & Meet Cutes*

**Donut Fall in Love Series**
*Donut Fall in Love*
*The Stand-Up Groomsman*

**Weddings with the Moks Series**
*Four Weddings to Fall in Love*
*Three Reasons to Run*
*Two Friends in Marriage*

**Chu's Restaurant Series**
*The Sitcom Star*
*The Reluctant Heartthrob*

**Kwan Sisters/Fong Brothers Series**

*Grumpy Fake Boyfriend*

*Mr. Hotshot CEO*

*Pregnant by the Playboy*

*Bidding for the Bachelor*


**Cider Bar Sisters Series**

*Her Big City Neighbor*

*His Grumpy Childhood Friend*

*Her Pretend Christmas Date* (novella)

*The Professor Next Door*

*Her Favorite Rebound*

*Her Unexpected Roommate*


**Holidays with the Wongs Series**

*A Match Made for Thanksgiving*

*A Second Chance Road Trip for Christmas*

*A Fake Girlfriend for Chinese New Year*

*A Big Surprise for Valentine's Day*

**Baldwin Village Series**

*One Bed for Christmas* (prequel novella)

*The Ultimate Pi Day Party*

*Ice Cream Lover*

*Man vs. Durian*


**Chin-Williams Series**

*Not Another Family Wedding*

*He's Not My Boyfriend*